TILL DAPH DO US PART

WEDDINGS. FUNERALS. SLEUTHING.

PHILLIPA NEFRI CLARK

Till Daph Do Us Part

Paperback ISBN: 978-0-6488652-2-3
Hardcover ISBN: 978-0-6488652-3-0

Cover design by Steam Power Studios
Editing by NasDean.com

A QUICK NOTE...

This series is set in Australia and written in Aussie English for an authentic experience.

A PERFECT LITTLE TOWN

The township of Little Bridges was pretty at any time of the year with century old oak trees lining the main street and shopfronts colourfully painted to give a sense of olde-worlde charm.

On this spring afternoon people wandered about enjoying the warmth after a long, cold winter. In a small park, families shared fish and chips and locals stopped for a chat with each other. A peaceful, happy place.

Until a chilling screech filled the air.

Daphne Jones didn't have time to admire the scenery as she pursued a hooded figure across one of the 'little' bridges which was actually quite long, arching high above a slow moving, wide river.

"Uh…ah," She puffed and panted, and as she ran, attempted to remove her jacket, giving up when the gold buttons which had looked so smart in the dress shop refused to budge. Much as she wanted to believe she was breaking a sprinting record, she suspected it was for slowest not fastest runner.

It was far too hot to be doing this in business clothes and shoes with heels. Even low ones.

Reaching the highest point of the bridge, she saw the hooded figure dash onto the path along the river, glancing over their shoulder.

"Staap!"

Daph, you sound like a banshee.

If she didn't hurry up, she'd lose any chance of catching the criminal. Why was nobody else around to help? John hadn't answered her rushed phone call.

She flew past a group of women, squeaking a plea to call the police but all she heard in return was a comment about how tight her clothes were. Followed by laughter. Well, at this rate she'd be as skinny as they were in minutes. She forced down the hurt feelings. No time for self-pity.

On the flatter surface of the path, Daphne sped up. Every step squeezed her toes and jarred her ankles but she wasn't letting them get away. Not away from her and most certainly not away with murder!

As the path wound under the trees, the shade brought immediate relief from the heat. But the further she went, the denser the undergrowth.

"No, no, no!" She was going to lose the hooded figure.

Heart pounding, she rounded a curve and with a sickening thud ran straight into the person she'd pursued, knocking them both to the ground.

Daphne got to her knees and then to her feet just before the other person, who pulled the hood back.

Daphne's mouth dropped open. "You."

"Me. And now you know who I am."

A few days earlier...

"I HAVE the great pleasure of announcing our newlyweds—Mr and Mrs Tanning! Please put your hands together to congratulate them." Daphne Jones frowned and crossed out the line she'd quoted in a notebook on her lap. "Needs more oomph. Not quite right, is it, love?"

When she got no response, Daphne glanced at her husband, John, who was driving. His focused expression was familiar as the car slowed. New town ahead. He needed to concentrate.

Daphne was terrible with navigation so didn't offer to find the road to the caravan park. Instead, she closed the notebook and put that and her pen into a large floral patterned handbag on the floor near her feet. She'd fix up the speech in no time once she'd met with the bride and groom this afternoon.

John checked the side mirrors and flicked on the indicator as they approached a large sign pointing down a side street with the words 'Little Bridges Caravan and Camping Ground'.

A tingle of excitement fluttered in Daphne's stomach and she couldn't help smiling as the car, towing their caravan, turned the corner. This was a dream come true. Travelling with their own caravan. Her new career helping people celebrate the happiest and saddest times in their lives. And watching John relax as he unwound from a lifetime of running a busy real estate agency.

John drove through a wide entry and soon was pulling the car over to one side of a long driveway. He turned off the motor and grinned.

"Made it, doll!"

"Of course we did! Another wonderful place to discover."

"I'll pop into the office over there and find out where our site is."

Daphne gazed around after he left. It was a quiet time of

the year for tourists, in between school holidays, which made booking their sites easier than during busy season. With her new line of work, she had a well-planned itinerary right through to next autumn, and even managed to factor in a couple of breaks when they'd go home to River's End for a week or two.

Once John returned with hand drawn directions, they followed a dirt road past the office until they reached an open area not far from a long row of trees. He deftly backed the caravan into the allotted space.

Out of the car, Daphne stretched and breathed deeply of the country air. "Is that the river?" She didn't wait for an answer. John was already unshackling the car and would be busy for a while setting things up the way he liked, so she headed in the direction where she'd caught a glimpse of water.

There were no other sites between theirs and a buffer of gum trees. Beyond the gums, a row of willows dipped their branches into a wide, slow moving river. The town peeked through trees and bushes on the other side and Daphne couldn't wait to explore. She hurried back to John.

"Do you think we should drive to town? Or walk?"

John had backed their large sedan next to the caravan and was working on connecting the power. "Bit busy at the moment."

"Yes, but when we've settled in. It looks so pretty!"

He got the plug in at last and finally gave his attention to Daphne. "You are so pretty, doll. Look at you. All excited about being here." He kissed her forehead. "Let's sort Bluebell out and then we'll go for a drive."

From the first moment Daphne set eyes on their caravan, Bluebell was its name. It might be older in style and not as flashy as some of the new ones they came across, but every inch of Bluebell had been lovingly restored and improved.

The interior was as modern as one would wish for with every convenience that could be fitted into the small space. But it was the outside, with its vibrant blue colour and touches of white in contrast which drew attention wherever they went.

'Sorting' Bluebell out took an hour. John was particular about his routine after settling at a new ground. Inspect the exterior including the tyres for any sign of wear or damage. Ensure the caravan was secure and properly plugged to power and water. Unravel the matching awning so they had an outdoor area ready to use.

Meanwhile, Daphne checked inside for anything which might have come loose. From a drawer she took out a handful of special things she always put away when driving. One of these was a snow globe and she turned it upside down then placed it onto the windowsill in the kitchen. The globe was a gift from their dear friends, Christie and Martin, and depicted their own little town of River's End.

She made up a shopping list. They'd used up the remainder of their food before leaving the last town and she needed to find a supermarket.

"Can't have John hungry after such a big drive." She added the ingredients for chocolate chip cookies as an afterthought. Nothing like them to go with a cuppa.

"Ready, love?"

Daphne ran a loving hand over the door as she closed and locked it after climbing out. "We'll be right back."

LITTLE BRIDGES WAS A DELIGHTFUL TOWN. Daphne longed to take a leisurely stroll around the shops but John reminded her she had an appointment. She'd come back tomorrow, after the wedding. They located a supermarket and as they wandered, John added a few items to the list. Daphne made sure he didn't notice her put the packet of biscuits back on the shelf. He loved her homemade ones much more and she'd bake them after meeting with the happy couple-to-be.

"I'll unpack, love." Daphne piled bags onto the small counter in the caravan. "Then I'll make us a quick sandwich before getting changed."

"No, you get changed and I'll do this." John opened the first bag. "I thought I might cook outside tonight on the grill. Maybe take a picnic blanket down near the river to eat."

"You are so romantic." Daphne kissed his cheek. "I might be a bit distracted though, depending on this meeting." She squeezed past him to go to the bedroom. "You know I do like to practice a bit before the ceremony."

"You can practice all you want. Have you seen the chocolate biscuits?"

He'd noticed. Of course he would.

"All that processed stuff isn't good for you, John Jones. And not nearly as nice as the ones I make." She peeked back to the kitchen. He was holding up the packet of chocolate chips in one hand and flour in the other with something which surely wasn't a grimace on his face. He must be imagining how delicious they were. "Keep those out, love. I'll make a batch once I'm back."

"Um, no need, Daph. You have enough to do today."

How sweet of him. "I always have time for you. You and homemade cookies."

A NOT SO PERFECT FAMILY

At exactly three minutes to two, Daphne waved to John as he drove away. He'd dropped her outside the home of the bride-to-be, Lisa Brooker. And a monster of a house it was with multi-levels, columns and balconies. Almost something out of a glamour magazine. It took up the full width of the end of a dead-end road.

She straightened her jacket. "Deep breath, Daph." Meeting her clients always got her heart beating a bit faster. Bookings for her officiant services were usually done through the fancy internet portal on her website so she rarely met a couple more than a couple of days before their wedding. There were always phone and often video calls between first contact and first meeting, but still, she never ceased to be amazed by how different some people were in person than she'd expected. She tightened her grip on the soft-sided briefcase John bought her as a Christmas gift last year and lifted her head. Time to get to work.

Stained glass double doors swung open before she'd climbed the half dozen stairs and a man stepped out.

"Mrs Jones?"

"Why, yes. But its Daphne. Please, call me Daphne, or Daph." She reached the man, who was about her age and dressed in a sombre black suit. As if in mourning. She pushed the silly thought away as he extended his hand to shake.

"Lisa and her mother are in the garden if you'd like to come with me." He closed the door behind her as she stepped into a foyer with a sweeping staircase to the next level. "I'm Lisa's father. Bob."

The house was perfect. It might have been a display home with movie stars being photographed on its deep sofas. A wide hallway led past open rooms, all in white with timber floorboards and cowhides scattered around. She sniffed. Fresh paint smell.

"This is a lovely house."

"Not looking forward to it being overrun with guests tomorrow." He walked faster than Daphne and she had to hurry to keep up, her heels tapping on the boards. They cut through a huge country kitchen where two women stopped talking to stare at her. She smiled and offered a small wave which was met with frowns. Oh, dear. This wasn't giving off the vibe of a happy home.

After crossing a casual living room complete with an enormous television, pool table, and pinball machine, they stepped through a sliding door onto a vast timber deck. It wrapped around the back of the house, disappearing beneath a roof where a built-in spa bubbled away near a tropical themed bar area. Steps led to a path around a resort style and sized swimming pool behind clear fencing. A shirtless man in his thirties was polishing the tiles around the pool on his hands and knees.

Beyond this, the path split, one way leading to a beautiful, rose-bordered garden where a handful of people worked on creating a reception space.

"It isn't good enough, Mother!" A wail filtered through a trimmed thick hedge along the other part of the path. "I wanted lilac. Not purple. Not pink. Lilac!"

Bob shook his head and muttered. "I want. I want."

An open wrought iron gate split the hedge in two. On the other side, more wedding preparations were underway. About one hundred white chairs, half on each side of a purple carpet, faced a partly-built, circular podium large enough for Daphne, and the bride and groom. Behind it, an elderly man attempted to connect parts of a mesh backdrop together. Covered with artificial flowers, it looked more awkward than heavy but it towered over the poor man who barely kept it upright.

"Excuse me. Always something to fix." Bob sprinted to help the other man. "Dad, really? Told you to wait."

One thing Daphne had learned from her few months as a celebrant was that weddings really did bring out the best and worst in people. Most of her clients so far were lovely. Nervous sometimes. But always polite and respectful of her role. A role they'd asked her to fill and paid her quite well to do.

As she stood on the path, alone, gazing at the scene before her, an odd sensation fluttered in her stomach. One that had nothing to do with how quickly she'd eaten her lunch earlier.

An inkling of unease.

A box of ribbons and bows sat open on one of the chairs and this was where the bride and presumably her mother stood. Lisa Brooker had her hands on her hips. For some reason Daphne had expected a woman in her early twenties but Lisa was perhaps ten years older than that. Her face, although pretty, was red with rage as she glared at the older woman holding up a bow.

"But, dear, this is a pleasant colour and will look nice on the chairs."

"Are you quite insane?" There was the wail again. "This is almost the same colour as my previous wedding. I cannot be married again using the same colours!"

"Then don't get married again! Stop putting your dad and I through this!" her mother snapped.

Lisa put a hand on her chest, her voice sad. "I thought you wanted me to be happy. Maybe I'll just elope."

"But Lisa—"

"No but anything. If you want this wedding to go ahead, send them away and find me the right ones. Oh. Hello." Lisa spotted Daphne. "Who are you?"

"I'm Daphne Jones, your wedding celebrant."

The change in Lisa was immediate. She smiled and hurried to shake Daphne's hand. "As you can see, things are a mess. People don't listen to instructions."

"I'm sure it will all come together."

Lisa's mother stared into the box and Daphne's heart sank. The older lady was crying. She found the spare clean handkerchief kept for such emergencies and skirted around more chairs, not brave enough to step on the purple carpet.

"Hello, dear. I'm Daphne." She used her calm and supportive voice as she held the handkerchief out. "Weddings are such emotional times."

"This is my mother, Margaret. She cries a lot."

Daphne hadn't noticed Lisa follow her. The younger woman grabbed a handful of bows from the box.

"Well, what do you think, Daphne? A girl can't possibly use the same colours for consecutive weddings? Can she?"

Great. Asking the opinion of the one person who had to be all things to all people on these occasions. Daphne considered her response. If she agreed with Margaret, who wasn't her client, then the bride might have more of a meltdown. On the other hand, Lisa had already made her mother cry and in Daphne's opinion, the mother of the bride should only cry happy tears on the day of the wedding. For that matter, how many weddings had there been already?

The eyes of both women drilled into her. Tears dripped down Margaret's cheeks. Lisa had a steely expression. There really was no way to win this one.

"Sorry I'm late! The boys at work wanted to give me a send-off and I couldn't say no."

Phew. Disaster averted.

A young man wearing shorts and a sleeveless checked shirt ambled down the purple carpet. Saved by the groom... perhaps? He looked barely out of school.

"What on earth are you wearing, Steve?"

With a lopsided grin, Steve Tanning put an arm around Lisa and kissed her. She put both hands against his chest and pushed him away, her nose wrinkled in disgust.

"How much have you had to drink?"

"Couple of beers. Can't blame a man for letting his mates buy him a drink the day before he gets hitched." Steve wasn't the least bit put out by his fiancée's response and wiped his hand on his shorts before shoving it at Daphne. "I'm Steve and you must be the wedding photographer. Except where are your cameras?"

"I told you we don't need one! Don't you listen either?"

"Best not to let me loose with a camera," Daphne said. "I'm Daphne Jones, your celebrant."

"Really? Thought you'd be younger."

Margaret gasped and covered her mouth with a hand. Bob's head shot up with a glare that would frighten most people, and Lisa turned even redder than before. Bob's father, who was weaving fine wire around two pieces of background, did nothing. Except grin to himself.

Daphne lifted her chin. "We're only as old as we feel."

Steve laughed. "Well, I feel twenty three and am twenty three so what does that say about me?"

A few replies came to mind but none of them mattered. Forcing down a sudden urge to turn and walk away and not return, Daphne stared straight at Steve without a word. He shuffled his feet and looked away.

The silence dragged until Daphne remembered she was here to help them get to their happiest day. Sometimes stress made people do and say things they normally wouldn't. These were nice people underneath.

"Shall we get started?"

A HAPPY MARRIAGE

"Now, doll, you make yourself comfortable and I'll pour you a nice glass of wine and let you relax a bit." True to his word, John had laid out a picnic blanket close to the river and made several trips back and forth to Bluebell to bring their dinner over. He'd taken one look at Daphne's set face when he'd picked her up from the Brooker house and decided to make her feel extra special tonight.

Not that it was hard to spoil his wife. Since their days as high-school sweethearts, he'd loved Daphne with his whole heart. She made him smile, gave him her full support in any endeavour, and knew when he needed space. Daphne was one of those rare humans who truly did care about other people's feelings and put their needs before her own.

"I didn't mean for you to do all the work." John helped Daphne down onto the blanket. Some days her knees weren't as good as they once were and she'd been on her feet all afternoon. "Thanks. This is a lovely spot."

John opened the cooler he'd carried across. Inside on a bed of ice was a bottle of wine, dessert, and glasses. He poured the wine and handed a glass to Daphne before raising his in a toast.

"To Daphne Jones. Celebrant extraordinaire."

She touched her glass to his but didn't take a sip and to his dismay, began blinking rapidly. Since she'd got into the car, she'd said little and when she had spoken, her voice was strained. He reached for her hand and squeezed it until she looked at him.

"Tough day at the office?"

Her lips were pressed tight against each other. John took both glasses and set them on the lid of the cooler, then held his arms open. In an instant she'd shuffled close enough to lean against his shoulder and he closed the hug.

"I don't want to cry." Her words were muffled and he loosened his arms a little to better hear her. "Not worth crying over rude people."

"True. But sometimes a good cry makes you feel better."

They stayed like that for a few minutes until Daphne's heart stopped pounding against his chest and was once again a normal beat. She hadn't cried but the rims of her eyes were red when she straightened. He handed her back her glass and this time she took a sip.

"Why don't you fill me in while I serve dinner?"

"Shall I help?"

"Nope." He opened the picnic basket and drew out a foil wrapped platter. "Went fishing in the river. Thought you'd like some of my world-famous fish tacos."

"You made all of this?" Daphne sniffed the air as he unwrapped the platter. "Why do you look after me so well?"

"Hey. No tears now!" John leaned over and kissed Daphne's cheek. "Tell me what happened."

"You know I don't take offence easily but the groom was not pleasant. Nor the bride, nor her father and even her grandfather. No lilac and past weddings and my age." The words tumbled over each other.

John shot her a look. "Your age? What has that got to do with anything. Or anyone?"

"The groom said he didn't expect me to be so old. That's after he mistook me for the wedding photographer. And nobody told him off."

"Wait on, love. The groom said that?" His chest tightened. Why would anyone say such a thing?

"He did. He's so young, John. Twenty three but he acts a lot younger. Turned up after going to the pub with his mates. In shorts and old boots."

"Age is no excuse for rudeness. So, they're a very young couple?"

Daphne took a minute to answer, enjoying a mouthful of the white wine before shaking her head. "Lisa, the bride, is thirty two. Now I'm not one to judge, and that age difference might not matter when both people are sensible, but the way they behaved today was immature. Lisa yelled at her mother a few times over silly things like the wrong colour bows for the chairs."

After filling a plate for Daphne, he started piling food onto his. "Maybe you've been lucky so far. Every wedding has been wonderful and you've come away thrilled to bits. Do you think they're just nervous?"

"Him, I can understand although he didn't even act as though tomorrow is his big day. But Lisa knows what to expect. This is her third wedding."

"I beg your pardon?"

"Only time I felt a bit sorry was when her mother told me she'd lost two husbands." Daphne put down her wine glass and picked up her plate.

John had it on the tip of his tongue to point out that if

Lisa Brooker was really so unpleasant her previous husbands may have had reason to divorce her.

"Nobody should be a widow so young." Daphne lifted a taco. "You're so clever, love. I'm starving." She took a bite and closed her eyes with a moan and then a smile.

Twice widowed and now about to marry again. John couldn't imagine marrying three times in a few years. With a bit of luck the Tannings would enjoy a long life together. Lots of time for them to annoy each other rather than ganging up on his wife or any other unsuspecting folk.

SAM, SHANE AND STEVE

A wonderful evening by the river, listening to the birds settle for the night, watching the sun set with the man she loved was enough to leave Daphne in a calm state of mind. Ready to begin again. She'd slept well after deciding not to work on the ceremony while upset. After breakfast and a nice cup of tea, Daphne had taken her notebook and gone for a walk where it was quiet beneath the willows.

She spent an hour tinkering with the words and then rehearsed until everything clicked into place in her mind. Despite their behaviour, Lisa and Steve had helped her out by having their vows typed and ready. She'd had them practice a few times so the whole event wasn't a complete shock, but whether Steve would remember was another thing. He'd definitely had a few beers and by the time they'd finished, he looked more interested in sprawling on the grass than standing in position.

Her last job before dressing for the event was to transcribe her most important notes into the ceremony book. Here she kept every service she did and she loved the look and feel of the bound and engraved book. When she'd been little, her mother had a diary with her name engraved on the front. It was forbidden to touch, which made it all the more mysterious. Mind you, it had a combination lock so was quite safe from the prying eyes of small children.

When John drove up the street to the Brooker house, Daphne's stomach churned and her hands shook so she held them tight within each other on her lap. This wasn't good, this feeling of dread in her gut.

Marry them and leave. It is only an hour until the ceremony. You can do this.

Daphne's life growing up was tough and she'd learned to talk herself into a better mindset when the old feelings of anxiety emerged. One day she'd talk to someone professional but most of the time she could talk reason to herself.

"Daph? You okay, love?" John stopped the car a short walk from the driveway, which overflowed with cars. "Would you like me to hang around?"

Yes! Except, no.

"You're so sweet. But I'm fine. And in exactly," she checked her watch, "two hours, I'll be waiting here and there will be a newly married couple in town."

A kiss or two and a check in the mirror later and Daphne was forcing her feet forward. The sense of dread hadn't lessened but at least she could concentrate on action rather than worrying.

She decided to go around the house first and take a look at the final set up in the garden. Then she would find the bride and go over any last minute questions. People were mingling in the reception area. It was bright and beautiful with lots of lilac and white decorated tables and chairs. There was a spot for the band who were going to play for the afternoon and white aproned catering staff busied themselves unpacking plates and glasses.

Half a dozen or so young men in suits took turns

drinking champagne directly from a bottle. One of them was Steve. Daphne raised her eyebrows but kept going. It was none of her business.

A handful of guests were already seated for the wedding. It was quiet here apart from soft piped music and hushed conversation. Daphne smiled at those who glanced at her and inspected the podium. The purple carpet was gone, replaced by one closer to lilac. Each chair was covered with white fabric decorated with lilac bows. Lisa had got her way. The podium itself had a couple of large vases of flowers. The backdrop of greenery was wound with lilac coloured artificial flowers, and although it looked ready to fall with a gust of wind, it did provide a pretty background. She stepped onto the podium and faced the audience. This was a nice sized area so no need for a microphone. Her voice would carry to the back.

As more people trickled in through the gate, Daphne returned to the house.

"Mrs Jones." Margaret carried a tray of champagne glasses out of the kitchen. "Would you like a glass?"

"Daphne. Thank you but no. Best I keep a clear head."

"Someone should. I apologise for everyone's behaviour yesterday. You were spoken to quite rudely."

"Weddings sometimes put people on edge. No need to worry."

"The problem is Lisa's choice of husbands."

Daphne didn't know how to answer, so kept her mouth shut.

Margaret handed the tray to someone going past and looked over her shoulder before continuing in a hushed tone. "Steve is nice enough, of course. But I keep thinking Lisa is trying to find someone just like her first husband. She loved him so much."

"How awful for her to lose two husbands. Is Steve like her first one, then?"

"Like him? They were cousins. Same as her second husband. Lots of big families around here and all three men she's chosen to marry were related to each other."

Daphne clambered for an appropriate response, but only came up with, "Did they both have a genetic disease? I mean, to die so young? And related."

Stop babbling, Daph.

Margaret didn't blink an eye. "No. Actually, they both had accidents. Sam was electrocuted and Shane fell off a ladder. Terrible accidents. Steve's family won't even attend the wedding because they somehow blame my Lisa."

"Oh goodness. What a shame. Best to keep Steve in bubble wrap!"

Aware she was at risk of going from bad to worse with her words, Daphne excused herself and found a bathroom where she locked herself in and fanned her face. She grabbed her phone from her bag and dialled John.

"Love? You okay?"

She whispered. "Yes. But Steve is the third in his family to marry Lisa."

"Unusual."

"Sam, Shane, and now Steve. Electrocution and a bad fall."

"Must have been bad. I mean if the poor bloke died."

"Yes! Exactly. And his family don't approve. Do you think she's one of those black widows, John? What if Steve is next? Should I refuse to marry them?"

Even as she said the words, Daphne knew she was overreacting. The upset from yesterday must have clouded her judgement. Good thing she'd not accepted the glass of champagne, although perhaps she should. It might calm her nerves a bit.

"Daph? Take a deep breath and pull yourself together. It

won't be long and then I'll be there to pick you up. What if we go into town for dinner tonight?"

She gazed at her reflection. Her eyes were too wide open. Startled. John was right. Take a breath and stop seeing things that weren't there.

"Sounds lovely. Dinner with my husband."

"Are you feeling a bit happier?"

"I am. Thank you, love."

"Only ever a call away. See you in a bit."

Daphne switched her phone to the silent setting and pushed it to the bottom of her bag. A glance at her watch made her heart jump. Time to check on the bride.

"You can do this, Daph." She smiled at her reflection. "Everyone is counting on you to make this a perfect ceremony and you can. You are special, and have a good heart."

With no further ado, Daphne opened the door and strode out.

A SHORT MARRIAGE

Fifteen minutes past schedule, the bride emerged through the open gate and walked down the aisle. Lisa gripped her father's arm and took care with her footing. If she'd had too much champagne then she was a good match for the groom. Short of doing a breathalyser test, Daphne couldn't judge their exact state and decided if they couldn't manage their vows then she'd call for a postponement. People had to be of sound mind when taking such a big step and she was the one who had to make these moments flawless.

Her job was to ensure their ceremony was perfect.

As perfect as a wedding with only one side of the family present, plus the groom's large group of semi-inebriated friends, and a demanding third time bride could be.

What could possibly go wrong?

Her concerns were unfounded and the ceremony, including the vows, went as planned.

As the final words were spoken, Daphne crossed her fingers beneath the ceremony book. Lisa had made her declaration first, a mix of old and new they'd chosen themselves. Now, Steve finished his part of the vow.

"Forever together, sick or well, rich or poor, until death do us part!" he finished with a flourish. And should have stopped there but as he slipped a wedding band onto Lisa's finger, he leaned closer with a grin and in a loud whisper, "You before me, darl. Given the age difference."

Lisa stepped back and the colour drained from her face as she snatched her hand away.

A stunned silence from the guests at the front was followed by queries of "What happened?" "What did he say?" from further back. Bob's mouth had dropped open and the expression of fury on Margaret's face was enough to scare anyone.

This could turn ugly fast. Daphne closed her book with a loud, "I pronounce you husband and wife. Steve, you may kiss Lisa."

For a moment it was more likely Lisa would storm off the platform. Steve gave her a lopsided smile. "Sorry, darl. I'm so nervous. Love you to the moon and back."

The anger in Lisa's eyes drained away and then she threw herself at Steve and they kissed.

"Let me introduce the happy couple, Steve and Lisa Tanning!"

Daphne raised her hands and the guests stood, clapping. And some whistling from Steve's friends. The newlyweds stopped kissing and joined hands and moved into the audience, leaving Daphne alone on the platform to pack away her things.

"Bet you're pleased that's over."

She jumped. Lisa's grandfather glowered at the backs of the happy couple.

"Always nice to see a couple married." She said in the cheeriest tone she could summon.

He turned his gaze onto her. "You have no morals marrying them two. No conscience. Shame on you."

The book slipped from Daphne's fingers, hitting the floor with a thump, notes falling here and there. Her mouth formed a question which couldn't come out, so tight was her throat. What did he mean? Why was he angry with her? Did he hate Steve so much he thought the world should conspire to stop the marriage of two grown adults?

"There you are, Dad." Bob appeared through the crowd. "Time for photographs."

"Not with me." The older man shook his head and pushed past his son, disappearing in a moment behind the backdrop he'd helped build.

"Dad, wait on!" Bob sighed. "Sorry about that. Dad is losing his faculties and can't remember his own name half the time."

Daphne didn't know his name but didn't care to ask.

"Nice ceremony, Mrs Jones. Will you stay for a glass of champagne?"

Her voice returned with a bit of a squeak. "I need the couple to sign their marriage certificate."

Bob nodded. "Of course. I'll go and find them. And thanks for being such a good sport. Can't imagine anyone else putting up with the behaviour of my family yesterday. And that little rat's comments at the end of the vows."

It took Daphne a minute or two to compose herself once he left. She collected the fallen notes and her book, packed everything back into her briefcase and then stepped off the podium. The dread was back in her stomach and she had to remind herself this was almost over. Sign the certificate and other papers and then walk away and never return.

NOTHING WAS THAT SIMPLE.

The signing table had been forgotten about, so space was hastily made in the middle of the gifts table. Daphne stood back as gifts were moved to one side by Margaret and staff. Quite a number were already open. A set of crystal glasses, placemats, toasters. Photo frames. Cutlery. And lots of envelopes, probably containing cash or gift cards. If this was the third wedding in a few years, some guests might have run out of ideas.

Daphne handed her phone to Margaret and asked her to take a few images of herself with the couple she could add to her officiant website. Once the table was dressed with some flowers, the happy couple sat and signed, stopping often for photos and kisses while their bridal party drifted away to a bar.

Once finished, Steve joined his friends for another drink and Lisa's bridesmaids returned with a bottle of champagne. Hopefully, none of them were driving later. Not that this was her concern.

Daphne made it as far as the back of the deck when Margaret caught her.

"Have you seen Bertie?"

"Bertie?"

"Bob's father."

Bertie Brooker, Bob Brooker. Steve, Shane, Sam. Did every family in Little Bridges keep to an alphabetic theme naming their children?

"Last I saw him was right after the ceremony. He went in the other direction from the guests. Behind the backdrop."

"Oh dear. He's been known to try and cross the river at the back of the property. We'll have to search for him."

By 'we', Daphne sincerely hoped Margaret meant 'they'. Finding a rude and grumpy man was not on her to-do list.

"Marg? Still can't find Dad so we're heading to the river."

Bob called from near the gate. He had a group of guests with him, some carrying full glasses as though they were going on an excursion. "Can you search closer to the house?"

Margaret waved in response.

Steve and his friends followed Bob. Just before the gate, Steve stopped, reached into a pocket and removed a phone. He answered the call as the others went on ahead.

"My husband will be here to pick me up soon. I can look around out the front if you like." Daphne said.

"Yes please. I have to help the others." Margaret hurried off in the direction of the reception area and Daphne breathed a sigh of relief.

She wasn't waiting to be stopped again and took a short cut through the house, diverting to use the restroom. The place was deserted and her heels echoed on the floorboards in the long hallway. There were family photos all the way along, some on the wall and others in frames on side tables. Lisa's previous weddings to two men who resembled Steve. Bob and Margaret's wedding which made them look as though they'd not aged a lot. Bob as a young man holding a trophy aloft. No, that wasn't Bob but Bertie. The next photo showed him crossing a finishing line in a running race.

"Probably ran to the river to get away from the wedding." She grumbled. Outside again, Daphne glanced around. "Bertie? Are you out here?" He didn't answer and there was no sign of movement.

The driveway and the street was like a carpark with cars and flatbed Utes parked at angles on verges. Four-wheel-drives lined up in rows. Half the town must be attending. Except the Tanning family.

A large white van was parked on the lawn. Its back doors were wide open and a young man, carrying a crisp white apron, emerged from its depths just as Daphne went around it, startling them both.

"Oh my! Sorry." Daphne laughed. He glowered at her and slammed the doors, then swiftly pulled the apron over his head before striding away. Poor thing must have spilled something over himself and was embarrassed. His shirt, now covered with the top of the apron, had wet splashes on it.

Daphne took a minute to send a text message to John, then found herself a spot where she'd see him drive down the street. Time to think about dinner tonight. Somewhere nice with a glass of wine and a laugh about the events of the day.

When John appeared in the distance she was well and truly over standing around. The car was almost close enough to see his face when a cry from the house made her turn and look. It sounded like a woman in pain. And again, this time the voice was recognisable.

Lisa.

And she shrieked one word over and over.

Steve.

THREE TIMES A WIDOW

Daphne's head shot back towards the street where John was searching for a place to stop.

"Steeeeeve!"

John waved.

She couldn't wait.

Daphne turned and ran towards the sound of shrieking.

"Daph? What's wrong?" John called.

"Emergency!" She managed to call over her shoulder as she wound her way around and between cars.

The screaming stopped. Daphne puffed her way past the house, her eyes darting to the reception area and then...to the pool area.

Lisa slumped on her knees near the swimming pool with her mother, staring into it. But at what? Daphne pushed on and went through the open gate.

Bob and a waiter were in the pool, fully dressed and drenched from head to toe as they paddled either side of someone floating in the water. Someone wearing the exact wedding suit Steve had been in. Sobs wracked Lisa and as Daphne stepped to the edge of the pool, she saw why.

Her heart almost stopped. It was Steve in the pool.

Face down.

"Turn him over!" Margaret cried.

A third man jumped in, stirring up the water. Between the three, they managed to rotate Steve onto his back.

Daphne rummaged in her bag for her phone and rang John. She didn't wait to explain. "You need to phone an ambulance and let them know there is a drowning victim here. Give them my number if they want a contact." She hung up and shoved the phone into her pants pocket.

The men got Steve to the side of the pool. Daphne tossed her bag to one side and dropped to her knees, leaning over the edge to hold his arm as Bob and the waiter climbed out. Steve's eyes were open and staring straight at her. Lifeless. Beneath him, a cloud of red panned out, seeping into the shirt of the third man, who remained at his side. It was the man who'd been polishing the tiles yesterday.

Bob virtually pushed Daphne aside in his haste to grab Steve and she plonked onto her behind. She shuffled out of the way as the men lifted Steve onto the tiles. On the far side of the pool, a small red mark marred the pristine white edge above the water.

"Doll, are you okay?" John was there, his hands strong under her arms as he helped her get to her feet. "Are you hurt?"

She shook her head, words unable to find their way out.

"There's an ambulance coming." Arm around her shoulders, John guided her a few feet away, scooping up her bag. Daphne looked at the hand she'd held Steve's arm with. It was red with his blood. She yanked her jacket off.

More people piled into the area and a woman announced she was a nurse and asked everyone to step back. She began to work on Steve, snapping orders at Bob and the other men to help her position him.

"We need an ambulance!" Margaret screamed.

"On its way." John answered. "Perhaps people could move their cars to make a way through for it."

A few guests took off in the direction of the street.

"Daph? I need to move ours as well. Do you want to come with me?"

She shook her head again.

"I've got your bag and jacket. You'll be here?"

How could she leave? Less than an hour ago she'd pronounced Steve married to Lisa. He'd been rude and stupid but nonetheless was a living, breathing person. How on earth had he ended up in the pool of all places?

Lisa collapsed in a heap, letting out loud, heaving sobs. Margaret patted her back but gazed at Steve with a vacant stare. Three times a widow. Something snapped Daphne out of her shock. Surely this wasn't possible. Three men from the same family all meeting with lethal accidents when married to the same woman. Something was terribly off. She narrowed her eyes to memorise the scene.

A large swimming pool surrounded by tiled flooring. A handful of sunchairs. Two buildings on the opposite side with their doors facing each other. The first had a sign 'change room'. The other was smaller and closed up. This building had a tap at the front with a short hose snaking off to one side. Clear pool fencing and gate surrounded the area. There were a lot of people standing outside the fence, while inside, the attempt to resuscitate Steve continued.

Bob joined his wife and daughter, water streaming down his clothes. The waiter stood apart, his hands clenching and unclenching and his teeth chattering.

Daphne hurried for the change room. She pushed the door open. A shelf against the far wall held a variety of folded towels and Daphne collected a selection, hugging them against her chest as she closed the door behind herself.

The door to the other building suddenly opened, revealing a glimpse of pool cleaning equipment and tins of paint before a man stepped out and shut then locked the door.

He slid keys into his shorts pocket as he saw her and what she carried.

"Good idea." He held out his hands and Daphne noticed he was also drenched. It was the other man who'd been in the pool. The one polishing the tiles yesterday. "I'll hand these out."

She let him take them. At least he had a shirt on if sopping wet with streaks of Steve's blood. He tossed one of the towels over his shoulder and took the others to Bob and then the waiter. The latter he spoke to and patted on the back and after a minute, the waiter nodded and left the pool area.

Some of Lisa's friends got her back on her feet and led her away. Margaret still stared at Steve. At the people working on him. All for nothing for he was gone.

"I have to find Bertie." Margaret announced to nobody.

"Let me help." Daphne touched Margaret's shoulder. "He wasn't at the river?"

"River? I don't know. Everyone came running when Lisa…"

"Come on, there's nothing we can do here. We'll find your father-in-law."

No sooner had they left the pool area they found him. He sat alone at a table in the reception area, back to the pool, drinking a beer.

"Dad! We looked everywhere for you."

Bertie stared at his beer. "Didn't look hard enough."

Margaret began to cry.

"What's wrong now, Mags?"

With a gulp, Margaret sat at the table. "Steve. In the pool."

Daphne hurried away to the bar and poured two glasses

of water. All the catering staff had vanished. Perhaps still looking for Bertie or else curious about Steve. She swallowed one glassful and took the other back for Margaret. "Here, sip slowly."

Bertie suddenly looked straight at Daphne. "You're still here."

She wished she wasn't. If John had arrived a moment sooner she'd be back at Bluebell. If this mean old man said one more nasty thing…

"Wanted to apologise. My head gets muddled sometimes when there's too much going on." He held out his hand to shake. "Will you accept my apology?"

A bit of Daphne's hurt drained away. "Oh, of course I will." She reached her hand out and gasped. She'd forgotten about the blood on it, now dried around her nails.

All three of them stared at her hand. "I need to wash this off."

She dashed off to the house and locked herself in the bathroom again. After scrubbing both hands as clean as she could, she dried them, talking to herself all the time.

"None of this is your problem, Daph. Take a deep breath and soon John will be back for you. We can go to Bluebell and I'll have a long shower and a cup of tea."

A siren wailed as she made her way outside. Guests congregated in the reception area, some seated, others walking aimlessly around. Some of the waiters stood at the bar not knowing what to do. One was the young man Daphne had startled at the van. He stared at her and a chill crept up her spine.

His shirt had been wet. He'd been getting a fresh apron.

"There you are, love." John put his arm around her shoulders. "Thought you were staying by the pool."

"There was blood on my hand. From holding his arm. Steve's."

"Do you want to go?"

"I don't think I can. Police might need a statement."

"But it was an accident."

They walked towards the pool area. The siren had stopped. The nurse still worked on Steve, her movements as precise as at the beginning, but her face lined with exhaustion. Blood formed a puddle around him which trickled across the tiles and dripped into the water.

"I don't believe it was accidental, John. And I think I know who is responsible."

"You're wrong!"

Daphne and John turned. Lisa swayed behind them, one of her friends keeping her from collapsing with an arm around her waist. Black trails of mascara cut through her makeup, all the way down her neck to the top of her white dress, leaving dark smudges along the lace.

"It was an accident. The tiles were polished for the wedding when the pool area was spruced up. Dad insisted everything look new again. He just slipped." Her voice broke. "Slipped. My poor boy." She had no more tears and there was an emptiness in her eyes which tugged at Daphne's heart. "All my poor boys."

With that, her eyes fluttered and she fainted.

SUSPECTS GALORE

Two paramedics wheeled past with a stretcher loaded with medical equipment. As Lisa fell to the ground, they stopped, confused.

Daphne pointed to the pool. "She's just fainted, we'll look after her. You need to go there."

John, with the help of Lisa's friend, managed to get her onto her side and she came around almost immediately.

"Just rest a minute. We'll get you some water." John said.

Margaret and Bertie hurried over and Bertie sank to the ground next to Lisa, patting her shoulder with soothing sounds. His eyes though flicked to the paramedics and the scene around the pool.

"What's going on?"

"I told you earlier, Bertie." Margaret said.

"I've lost my Steve, Gramps." Lisa lifted her head. "I'll never keep a husband, just like Dad used to say."

Daphne's ear pricked up. Who would say such a thing to their own child?

"He never meant it, sweetie," Margaret said. "You always got bored so fast. New toys lasted a day before you'd break them. You'd make a friend then decide they weren't good enough. But that was a long time ago."

John's mouth had dropped open and Daphne took his arm. "We might go and sit for a bit. If you are all okay here?"

Nobody answered.

Daphne was happy to find a table away from the pool and from the lines of worry on her husband's face, so was John. He reached for her hand.

"Are you doing okay? This must have been a shock."

"I'm fine now you're here, love." She drew in a deep breath and exhaled. "So much happened today and when I saw you driving down the street all I longed for was to have a shower and cup of tea and tell you all about it."

"Surely there's no need to stay though?"

"I know things."

"O...kay." He said.

"Suspects."

"But we don't even know if a crime's been committed. The poor young man may very well have slipped as the bride suggested."

Another siren sounded.

"I guess we'll find out." Daphne said.

John leaned closer. "Before, you said you knew who is responsible. Daph...what do you know?"

Daphne looked over her shoulder. Most people now stood in a semi-circle around the pool as the paramedics did their job, but a few guests and a couple of waiters remained in the reception area.

"Quick rundown, love. Not everyone approved of the wedding. For a start, there's none of Steve's family here." Daphne's eyes widened. "Oh goodness. Has anyone contacted his family?"

"Quite a few people are on their phones."

"This is terrible. Can you imagine not attending your

loved one's wedding and then they die?" She heard her voice rising and put a hand over her mouth.

"Stay here, doll." John went to the unattended bar and overfilled a glass of champagne. He returned and put it in front of her. "I know this is highly inappropriate given the circumstances, but there's only that or beer and I feel a little drink might settle your nerves."

Not one to drink during the day, Daphne wasted no time to sip the bubbly alcohol. It warmed her stomach. She'd not noticed how upset she was until hearing her tone change. Once she'd had a couple more sips—and didn't the champagne go down easily—she was ready to continue.

"Since stepping onto the property yesterday, I've observed a lot of strange behaviour, and honestly, some quite disturbing attitudes." She put down the glass and counted with her fingers. "Three men from one family all marrying the same woman within a few short years. And all three now deceased."

John nodded. "That is unusual."

"Quite. None of the groom's family in attendance."

"Families can be difficult."

"The groom himself was very rude to his bride during the vows."

"Not a good start to a marriage." John said.

"The bride's grandfather told me I had no morals by marrying them."

"Oh, love." John frowned. "What a dreadful comment."

"He did apologise later. Poor old soul seems to have dementia so I can't hold a grudge."

"You are the sweetest woman I know."

His words helped. They always did.

"Mind you, there was a lot of drinking going on before and after the ceremony. Which might have led to Steve slipping and falling into the pool." Daphne pressed her lips together.

"But you don't think it was an accident."

She didn't.

Police officers made their way to the pool, where paramedics were zipping Steve's body into a bag. Lisa was sobbing again, surrounded by her friends. Bob and Margaret stood back, silent. Bertie was nowhere to be seen again. Hopefully not another disappearance.

"Something strange happened. I was on my way to the street to wait for you and went past the caterer's van, surprising a waiter." Daphne said.

"Go on."

"He had wet patches on his shirt. And sleeves. And he was putting on a fresh apron."

"You think he got wet pushing Steve into the pool?" John asked.

She finished the glass of bubbles, surprised it was gone already.

"Should I get another?"

"Goodness, no thanks, love, you'd have to carry me out of here."

The paramedics pushed the stretcher out of the pool area, followed at a distance by Lisa and her friends. Her parents were with the police but Bob, arms folded and face set, watched the body of his ten-minute son-in-law wheel away.

"And that's another thing. According to Lisa, her father used to tell her she'd never keep a husband. Apparently as a child she became bored with friends and toys easily."

John looked in the direction Daphne discretely pointed. "That's her father and mother?"

"It is."

"Do you think he'd kill his daughter's new husband?"

"He needs to be on the list."

"List?"

"Suspects, John. I am keeping track up here," she tapped the side of her head. "Although it might pay to write it all down."

He gave her a slight smile. "Anyone else?"

"At least two more. Her mother didn't like Steve and she really wasn't happy yesterday about hosting another wedding."

"Not really a motive to kill someone."

"Tip of the iceberg, love. Tip of the iceberg. There's always more lurking beneath the snippets they let slip. And of course the obvious suspect is Lisa although I don't believe she did it."

"Bit odd to kill her new husband off only minutes after saying 'I do'." John glanced over Daphne's shoulder. "Think the police are heading our way."

Daphne scanned the reception area. The waiter was missing. He might be simply helping pack things away. Or he might have done a runner. She should have taken a photo of him the instant he became a suspect.

SUSPICIONS IGNORED

John didn't know what to do. Not knowing what to do was a worry. In a lifetime as owner and principal of River's End Real Estate, he'd encountered all kinds of folk and a myriad of situations. In the past couple of years, he and Daphne even had to deal with their house being broken into and treasured items destroyed by a fiend who was part of a conspiracy by a shady land developer. Despite all the turmoil, he'd always been able to keep a handle on his emotions, keep a cool head, and be there for Daphne.

This was different. As he sat at the table in a beautiful garden on a warm spring afternoon with his wife and a police officer, the situation was surreal. Daphne had been uncharacteristically nervous when he'd dropped her here. Perhaps nervous wasn't the right word. Uneasy. She had good instincts and was an excellent judge of character and today she'd been uneasy.

With good cause, so it turned out. Everywhere in view, people were in a daze. Some stood in small groups, others sat at tables or on the grass. Few spoke. The laughter and happiness expected at a wedding reception was non-existent. A second ambulance had arrived and one paramedic was checking Lisa while the other spoke to each guest to see if any of them needed assistance. What a dreadful way to end a wedding.

"Mrs Jones, we wanted a word, given your unique position as an outside observer." The young constable opposite John kept an eye on those around them, some who'd moved closer as though to listen in when he'd joined them.

"Of course, Constable McIntyre. And I have some information."

He took out a notepad. "Information?"

Now it was Daphne who gazed from group to group as if judging whether it was safe to speak. "I saw someone acting suspiciously earlier. A waiter."

"Suspiciously?"

She nodded. "He was in the catering van changing aprons. I noticed his shirt was wet in places, and his sleeves."

Constable McIntyre didn't write anything down. He stared at Daphne as she continued.

"This was a few minutes before Steve was found. He'd have had time to push Steve in and get changed. I assume poor Steve hit his head on the way in."

"The coroner will determine the cause of death in due course. This may well have been an unfortunate accident. Did you observe any odd behaviour from Mr Tanning prior to his death?"

"I've only met him twice. Both times he was unpleasant in the regard that he spoke before thinking. Whether that is true of him always, you'd need to ask someone better acquainted with him, but you tell me...is it odd to make a comment during your vows that you expect your wife to die before you due to her age?"

"Can't say."

"Going back to the waiter, I really think—"

"I'll look into it. What other observations do you have of the events of today?"

Daphne wasn't happy. The way she pressed her lips together was a giveaway to anyone who knew her. And John did. He reached a hand under the table and squeezed her leg and the corners of her mouth softened.

"There were a number of people unhappy with the couple getting married. Lots of people drinking too much before and right after the ceremony. And at least five suspects. Likely more once I've had a chance to catch my breath."

"I'd rather you don't look for suspects. That's our job. May I have your contact details?"

Through almost gritted teeth, Daphne told them where they were staying and exchanged her business card for one with his details.

The constable stood. "We'll be in touch if there is a need for a statement. How long do you plan on staying in Little Bridges?" He directed this to John, who also stood.

"For as long as Daphne wants to be here."

"Right. Well, thanks."

With that, the constable headed for Margaret and Bob. The latter had changed into dry clothes but his hair was still damp and sticking up at odd angles.

"John?"

Daphne's voice was strained and he immediately held his hand out.

"Can we leave now?"

"We certainly can." John helped her to her feet. Her face was pale and when they made their way to the front of the house, her arm in his, her steps were slow. He'd make sure she had a rest and some tea and even some of the packaged biscuits he'd bought on his way back to Bluebell earlier. She wouldn't mind for once.

The caterers were packing up, the back doors of the van open. Daphne tugged at John's arm.

"Let's wait a minute." They were a few metres away, between a row of bigger vehicles.

"Why, love?"

Two of the staff loaded glasses, plates and the like into the van. They finished and headed back towards the house, leaving the doors open.

In an instant, Daphne was off, scrambling into the back of the van. She was rummaging around before John knew what was happening. "Daph!"

She didn't listen and was in the depths of the van by the time he caught up. "What are you doing? You'll get caught."

"Then be a lookout."

A sudden bubble of laughter rose in his chest and he had to force it down. This was his girl at her finest. Following her instincts.

John turned to face the house. He'd give her time to do whatever it was she needed to do. After the couple of days she'd had, she deserved this chance. Daphne always did the right thing and he would back her one hundred percent.

"Anything?" He whispered over his shoulder.

"Hmm."

A procession of vehicles turned into the street. Four or five cars, one after another. Over at the house the paramedics were packing up their ambulances.

"My, oh my!"

"What?"

Silence again.

The cars slowed and one by one, pulled over to park. From the first car, four people emerged. A man and woman about his and Daphne's age, plus two young men. All wore an air of disbelief, of panic, and moved quickly towards the house.

42

"Um, Daph?"

"Almost done."

"Think Steve's family are here."

The catering staff headed directly towards them.

"Daph, get out. They're coming back."

"Almost done."

"I'm serious. You have to get out."

John took matters into his own hands. He made a beeline for the caterers, who between them were carrying a couple of tables. They squeezed through the cars and he blocked the way.

"Excuse me. Do you happen to know…um, where a nice place is in town for dinner?"

They stopped and stared at him as if looking at a crazy person.

"We're just passing through…for the wedding. Thought we'd go out tonight."

The first one went to push past and John stepped in front of him. "Whoops, sorry. Meant to go the other way. So, no suggestions?"

"Oh, there you are, John. Shall we go?"

Thank goodness.

John let them pass. The second person grinned and said, "Bell's Bistro. Most of us work there. Just off the main street."

Daphne appeared from around the end of a car and grabbed John's arm.

"Let's go." She whispered, tugging at him. He got the message. She'd found something important. They hurried away from the van, from the house, passing a long procession of people from the newly arrived cars.

"I need to speak to the constable again." She whispered.

"Looks like he'll have his hands full for a bit."

John ushered Daphne into the car just as Bob and Margaret and some of the other guests came around the side of the house to meet the newcomers head on. Everyone stopped for a second. Two seconds. And then the yelling and pushing began.

"What's happening?"

John closed her door and ran for his. Throwing himself in, he locked the car and started the engine.

"The other side have arrived and there's going to be a fight."

"Should we help?" Daphne craned her neck to catch a glimpse as John turned the car.

"Police are there."

"But I think we—"

"We, my love, are leaving. Enough of these people and this madness. I need you safe."

BLUEBELL'S BLESSINGS

Daphne didn't say a word all the way home. Her mind raced and a little bit of her heart broke. She'd wed those two and they'd not even enjoyed one day of married life. Her throat was tight and she knew if she spoke about them she would cry. John had been wonderful during the brief discussion with the constable who'd not believed a word she'd said. And he'd had her back when she'd got in the van.

"Here we are, love," John parked the car beside the caravan. "Time for you to have a shower while I make a nice cup of tea."

With a quick nod, Daphne climbed out and when John unlocked the door, was quick to climb the couple of steps to the cool and inviting interior of Bluebell. For a minute she paused in the kitchen, hands on the counter and eyes closed. Quiet. She could breathe again.

The boot of the car closed. John must be bringing her jacket and bag. Not ready to talk, Daphne closed herself in the cosy bathroom and stripped off. First stop tomorrow would be to locate a dry cleaner. She needed her clothes fresh again. No lingering smell of chlorine or…death.

The young constable didn't want her involved and he was right. She shouldn't interfere in police work. What she thought she'd seen was in her imagination, over-active from the shock.

She gulped.

Shower on, Daphne stepped under the water. The caravan carried its own supply so showers were normally short, but here, being hooked up at the site, she could afford the extra time to wash her hair and clean off the makeup and dirt and any trace of blood on her hand.

It isn't fair.

Not the way she'd been treated.

Or how Steve spoke to his bride during the vows.

The family arguing beforehand.

A young man's life cut short.

The perfect ceremony forever ruined.

Tears poured down her cheeks and she let out a sob. None of it was fair.

TWENTY MINUTES LATER, Daphne emerged from the bedroom in a short sleeved, floral blouse and soft, half-length pants. Pretty, cool, and comfortable to wear. She'd partly dried her hair then stopped to peer in the mirror.

"Are those greys?"

Holding up a strand, she almost bumped her nose on the glass trying to see.

"Time for a new highlight colour. What about bright blue?"

She'd normally straighten her curls but was in no mood

to bother. Let them curl. There was no sign of her earlier tears under a light application of makeup.

"There you are, doll." John was in the kitchen. "Shall we have tea in here? I've got it ready."

"Let's. Nice and cool inside." Daphne slid behind the table.

The table was booth-style, big enough for four diners. There was a plate of packaged chocolate biscuits in the centre and although Daphne disapproved of John's love of them, for once she didn't care to mention it. In fact, for once she was going to enjoy eating one. Or three.

They chatted over the first cup of tea about everything other than today. The weather, how pleasant the location was, and whether to go out for dinner or get take away.

"I'd really like to go out, if you feel like it." Daphne eyed off another biscuit. "Being somewhere happy, where people are laughing and happy would be nice."

"Agree. Did you want to try the bistro the waiter mentioned?"

"Didn't he say that's where most of them work? Maybe another night, John. Less reminder of what happened today."

"We'll go for a walk around town then and see what appeals. Do you care to share what you were doing in the catering van?"

"Oh! I almost forgot about it. I'll get my phone." She wiggled out. "I must have left it in my pants pocket."

Sure enough, it was in the laundry hamper.

"Sorry I dived into the catering van without a word." Back in her seat, Daphne tapped on the gallery. "Had to take the chance while nobody was there."

"Chance to do what?"

"Look for evidence, of course."

"Of course."

"I know Constable McDon't-get-involved wasn't going to

47

believe me so I got some proof." She handed the phone to John. "There's about ten photos. Tell me what you see."

The third chocolate biscuit made it to her mouth as John inspected the images, zooming in and scrolling from one to another.

"This one looks like a rolled up piece of cloth. Tablecloth?"

"Negatory. If you look closer you'll see a name tag."

John opened the case of his reading glasses and put them on, then enlarged the image. "I see it. Lloyd? So, an apron, not a tablecloth."

Daphne couldn't help smiling. "Yes! And it looks wet to me. See how part of it is darker than the rest?"

"You think this belonged to the waiter you surprised."

"I do indeed."

John grinned across the table. "Clever cookie. What about this photo?" He turned the camera. "What's that tub?"

In the corner of the van, almost hidden behind folded table and chairs, a white tub about the size of a large paint tin was pushed to the back.

"No idea. Cleaning stuff? Anyway, I thought it worth recording. The police officer thought I was a nosy old woman."

"Doll, no." John took her hand and squeezed. "He would have had a hundred things to worry about. Arriving to what looked like an accident but all those guests and family standing around and perhaps a homicide. Probably didn't know where to start."

Unconvinced, Daphne nodded. She knew what she knew. She just didn't know how to help. But the police had to see these photos.

"I'll quickly call the constable and let him know."

"Good idea. Then, how about we shelve all of this for

now? Would you like to know what I got up to while you were at the wedding?"

The way John's eyes lit up warmed Daphne's heart. He was so sweet, trying to distract her and excited about his news. She squeezed his hand back.

"I can't wait to hear!"

***

JOHN HAD a couple of projects on the go. Accustomed to working long hours and being active for his adult working years, the caravan life—as he called it—left him wanting more. He loved being on the road with Daphne, exploring Victoria and seeing her happy in her new career, but he couldn't fish all the time and needed his mind busy. Genealogy was a growing passion but what he had to show Daphne was something for them both.

He opened his laptop on the table. "I've been dabbling with this for a few weeks, mainly to keep our friends in River's End up to date with our travels."

Daphne shuffled closer, resting her head on his shoulder as he connected to the internet and then typed in an address. The screen changed and she sat bolt upright with a gasp.

"But…that's Bluebell!"

"Sure is."

"Is this a blog? Called Bluebell's Blessings?"

"Yup."

"You clever man! I love it."

For the first time today, John's spirits lifted. His girl was happy and he found himself grinning. "As I mentioned, the original idea was to keep our friends up to date. I've taken lots of photos of Bluebell," he moved to the 'gallery' page. "Inside and out."

Daphne squealed. "How did you make the living area look so big?"

"Found a neat little trick with my phone. Now here, on this next page, is our itinerary on the map of the state. At least, a rough outline, based on your commitments. And if you like, I can link this to your website. Gives potential customers a bit of insight into who you are as well as allows them to look here and see if you are already booked on a certain day."

Before John knew what was happening, Daphne threw her arms around him and planted a kiss on his cheek.

He laughed when she released him. "Take that as a yes."

"Yes. I'm so glad you're doing this. Not just for our friends or as something to look back on, but so you have something to do. I've worried a bit whether you would get too bored traipsing the countryside for me."

"Bored is not a state I could ever be in when you are involved. If there's one thing I've learned from being married to you for some forty years, Daph, it's that life always has a twist."

TWISTS INDEED

Those words of John's rattled around in Daphne's mind for a while. Life always had a twist. When she'd married her high-school sweetheart after they graduated, she'd relished the idea of raising a large family with him. The twist was trying to start a family for ten years before discovering it could never happen.

A cruel twist.

Daphne believed in silver linings though. They moved to the seaside town of River's End where John opened his business. For a long time they were foster parents and loved welcoming young ones into their hearts and home until more permanent arrangements were made. As a teen, local lad Martin Blake, who'd lost his own parents young and lived with his granddad, made it his business to help the Jones' out and befriend often troubled and confused kids who needed a new path. And even now, Martin spent time each year teaching at a camp for troubled teens.

A good twist.

Some of those foster children kept in touch while others stayed with the Jones' only long enough to tiptoe into

Daphne's heart before they were moved to their permanent homes. One in particular lingered in her memories and perhaps one day, they'd meet again.

Daphne was unsure yet how to view today's events. A twist indeed. Tragic. Unexpected. But was it murder? With the arrival of evening and having spent a couple of hours talking with John about Bluebell's Blessings, her earlier contention of foul play was a bit dented.

"What about this one?" John asked.

They wandered arm in arm after walking into town, following a path to the river and a bridge not far from the caravan which offered a short cut.

"This one is Mexican. Oh, but we had tacos last night." John said. "Looks like Italian up on the corner."

"Italian sounds ideal."

For a country town in the middle of Victoria, Little Bridges had a wonderful selection of eateries. They had planned to stay another two days, but that might change if the police needed them to be available for interviews. As long as they left by Thursday, they'd cover the distance to the next wedding with time to spare.

Once settled at a window table made cheery with a red and white checked tablecloth and matching candles, they chose from a small menu and John ordered a bottle of local red wine.

Daphne sighed and reached across the table for both of John's hands. "This is lovely. Thank you, love."

"I'm happy to see you smiling."

"Well, I feel much better. And seeing all the work you've put into Bluebell's Blessings filled my heart up."

John's face reddened but his eyes sparkled. He wasn't a man to expect compliments but deserved every one ever given. Over their lifetime together, he'd helped more people than Daphne could remember. The real estate agency sponsored local kids' sports as well as making a hefty donation each year to different local charities. He was a good man.

Two waiters moved a couple of tables to form a large one beside Daphne and John. They set it up for eight patrons and chatted the whole time.

"Didn't think they'd still come out tonight."

"Boss says they never cancelled but yeah, who'd go to a restaurant almost straight after what happened."

"Did you know him?"

"Steve Tanning? Went to school with him."

Daphne smothered a gasp as the waiters continued.

"Sorry, man. Are you okay?"

"Oh, we weren't friends. He and his cousins were part of the cool group. You know, the ones who think they're better than anyone else and push everyone else around. Can't say he'll be missed."

The conversation ended as they returned to the kitchen. Daphne leaned closer to John. "You heard that?"

"Would you like me to see if they can move us further away, love?"

"Further? Oh goodness, no. Right here is perfect."

Perfect to listen in and perhaps get some updates on the events after they'd left.

"Daphne, what are you thinking?" There was a touch of lament in John's voice.

She smiled as widely as she could. "Nothing at all. Here comes our wine."

By the time their wine was poured, the diners on the other table were settling in. Daphne decided to focus on her evening with John. They chatted about plans for the next day, which included a nice long walk around town and a visit to the local bookshop.

From the corner of her eye, it was impossible not to

recognise some of the faces from the wedding. Most were around the age of Bob and Margaret.

Daphne moved her chair a bit so she couldn't see them. A plate of garlic bread arrived and that gave her something yummy to concentrate on. More people arrived and before long, the restaurant was filled with laughter and talk. Exactly what she'd hoped for.

"They should have been arrested."

She wasn't going to listen. Daphne shuffled again, as close to the window as her chair would allow. But the man's voice carried and she couldn't very well put her fingers in her ears.

"Coming onto Bob's property and starting a fight."

"I suppose the police took their grief into account." A woman suggested.

"What about Bob and Margaret's grief?"

Nobody could have expected what came next.

Laughter.

Daphne and John turned as one. All but two of those at the next table were laughing. The ones who weren't amused were the oldest couple, a man and woman in their seventies.

"Come on, Pat and Gina. You know it's true." It was the first man. "They were horrified that silly girl of theirs wanted another go with a Tanning. Best thing for everyone if you ask me."

Gina frowned. "Be careful nobody outside this group hears you say so. A family feud is still no reason to wish harm on another. And he was only a boy."

Before they were caught listening, Daphne and John each grabbed another slice of bread. Their eyes met across the plate.

The first man continued. "Bertie will be happy. I reckon Lisa marrying into the family of his arch enemy started him going downhill. Nothing like a couple of good accidents to set things right."

Daphne shoved the bread in her mouth. She was getting tired of having to suppress gasps and really shouldn't be listening.

More laughter.

A waitress attended the other table and talk turned to selecting food and drinks. Seemed as though at least one of them already had quite a bit to drink from his loud-mouthed comments. Did he actually know something about the deaths of Sam and Shane?

What if he's the killer?

Oh dear. There she went again, thinking of Steve's death as murder. It wasn't her business and she wasn't about to make it her concern.

"John, I'm staying out of it. Promise."

"I know."

Their mains arrived and the table near them stopped discussing the wedding. The food was a delight and Daphne wasted no time enjoying it rather than worrying.

Before dessert arrived, she visited the restroom. As she washed her hands, the woman who'd been referred to as 'Gina' came in. She was a thin woman, heavy makeup covering deep wrinkles, wearing pearls and a fitted black dress. Their eyes met in the mirror.

"Don't believe everything you hear, dear."

Daphne tilted her head. "What do you mean?"

"I know you are at the next table. Saw you the minute we arrived. One of our party had a few drinks earlier from the shock of the events at the wedding, so don't think for one minute he is making sense."

There was nothing to say. Daphne dried her hands with a paper towel.

"You'll be leaving soon. On your way to the next town. No reason to dig around in our family history. Or in my family's town. So move on and forget about us." Gina said as if making small talk. "You were in such a rush to speak to the police at the wedding. Not a good look."

Well, well, well! Somebody wanted to hide something.

"I'm sure I have no idea what you are talking about. My husband and I are simply having dinner—"

"At the same restaurant half of Lisa's family are attending. Did my great-niece tell you we'd be here?"

"Lisa? Of course not. We just walked—"

"Either way, you aren't welcome. You played your part and now is the time to toddle along." Gina looked Daphne up and down, her eyes stopping on her stomach. "After your dessert of course."

It took a moment for Daphne to get the message but then ice filled her veins. She couldn't answer because Gina had left. Obviously, her visit to the restroom was designed to speak with Daphne. To insult Daphne. And warn her off.

Daphne lifted her chin. She might not wear pearls and a tiny little dress but she had a heart.

"And courage." Half-tempted to follow Gina and tell her some truths, instead, she straightened her top. "And manners."

CHANGE OF HEART

Dawn was John's favourite time of the day and since they'd embraced the travelling life, he'd managed to photograph some glorious sunrises. One day, he might put all of them into a book and publish it. For now it was a hobby to enjoy.

He wandered down to the river, a steaming cup of coffee in one hand and phone in the other. Daphne was still asleep, exhausted from the previous day. Once she woke, he'd make them a nice breakfast. Being able to spoil her a bit more these days was long overdue after her dedication to his needs for so long. His and their foster family over the years.

The sun peeked through the gums near the town. The river turned to gold.

John put his cup onto the grass and took lots of photos. Phone cameras today were every bit as good as a high quality camera and he loved the little tricks he was experimenting with to get the most out of every shot.

Birdsong filled the air. Magpies warbled. A family of kookaburras launched a cacophony of chuckles quickly elevating to their characteristic laughter. A flock of sulphur crested cockatoos screeched overhead as they swooped to see if John had anything interesting on offer.

"Come to the country, they said." John picked up his coffee. "It'll be quiet, they said."

He turned back. There was movement in Bluebell, a shadow crossing the kitchen window. He must have disturbed Daphne. For a moment he stopped, nursing the cup and sipping the coffee.

Their dinner last night was meant to help her unwind and move on from the trauma of the wedding. Instead, something happened to upset her more. He'd seen that woman called Gina follow Daphne to the restroom and leave first. Daph came back to the table a few minutes later, her eyes down. She forced a cheeriness he recognised as covering up hurt. On the walk back she'd said little and once in the caravan, headed to bed.

This mess with the accident yesterday, compounded by comments from the next table at the restaurant, all stirred Daphne up. Back when they were still in River's End, her friendships and sense of adventure dragged her into a few unusual situations. Mysteries she'd helped solve. She'd always been one to jump in. And more than once, John had asked her to stay out of other people's business. Just when she got too enthusiastic. But she had a way of seeing through lies and deception and if she really believed Steve was murdered, then John would back her all the way. Even if it meant getting a bit more involved than he was comfortable with.

"There you are!" Daphne opened Bluebell's door. "Kettle's on if you'd like another."

"Good morning. Yes, please."

She stepped back to let him in and he gave her a kiss on the cheek.

"John, do you mind if we go to the police station this

morning? I'd like to see if they can take my statement." Her voice was flat.

"If you'd like. Or we can wait for them to call."

With a shake of her head, she took John's cup and turned to the kitchen. "I thought if I can do the statement, then perhaps we can get going. To our next destination."

"Today?"

"I think it's best."

"Daph—"

"So, would you like eggs for breakfast?"

WHEN JOHN LET himself out of the caravan earlier, Daphne was awake. She'd heard the kettle boil and considered getting up to join him. But the thoughts in her head weren't ready for sharing and she had to find a way to deal with all of this without getting worked up and teary.

Gina had hurt her last night. Not only by insinuating Daphne was there to snoop around but the swipe at her weight.

Daphne turned on her back to stare at the ceiling. Her hands moved to her stomach. Where Gina had stared. It might be a bit more round than a few years ago, and she'd never fit into the figurative 'little black dress', but what business was it of anyone other than Daphne? And perhaps John, who was too sweet to ever comment on her growing waistline. Sliding her hands from under the blankets, she held them up. Her fingers were a bit thicker than they used to be although her long nails gave an illusion of length. But those hands were used for good.

In all the years she'd lived, Daphne had never concerned herself with fitness or being trim. Long ago, she'd decided her body would be what it wanted and she'd care for it to her best ability without obsessing. Enjoy her cookies sometimes but also love a good long walk. It all balanced up in the end.

Speaking of ends, she'd noticed her suit pants were a fraction tight when she'd donned them yesterday. Either they were shrinking with the regular dry cleaning, or she was spreading thanks to all the good food they enjoyed. A bit more walking might be the go. And walking away from this place was something high on her new list of priorities. There was no point staying where she wasn't welcome. John deserved better than the flow-on effect of nasty people. No, it was time to go.

Once dressed, Daphne put the kettle on in anticipation of John's return. Well accustomed to his pre-dawn wanders to take photos, it always gave her a few more minutes in bed and she appreciated how he tiptoed around so not to disturb her. She'd cook some eggs for them both then once the police station was open, she'd ask if she could do a statement today.

Don't run away, Daph. You're an adult now.

She held back a sob. No more tears. It was best they left now. More time to spend along the way to the next town. And get away from the upsetting events in Little Bridges.

NOT GOING ANYWHERE

C onstable McIntyre was apologetic but firm. "We're understaffed and working at capacity to investigate yesterday's incident. That and dealing with almost constant interruptions from…well, other parties, means we can't get to all the interviews just yet."

Daphne and John were at the counter in the police station. Behind the constable were three other police officers. Two spoke on the phone and one covered a whiteboard with notes. Sadly, a bit too far away for Daphne's eyes.

"If you really need to get to your next town, we can arrange an interview at another police station."

"I understand. It's just that I have some information you might find useful."

"Is it about the photos from the catering van we discussed on the phone? The photos you should not have taken?"

"Well, yes. And last night we overheard what sounded like inside knowledge of the deaths of Lisa's previous husbands." Daphne said.

"Didn't we talk about not getting involved?" There was no malice in his tone, only a touch of defeat. The young man was obviously tired. His eyes were a bit bloodshot and he looked as though he'd been up half the night.

Her initial assessment of him changed. There was nothing offensive or dismissive about him. He was right. They didn't need her help or her getting under their feet.

"Let me check if I have your details. One minute, please." He headed towards a desk.

"Daph? Why don't we stay a day or so. Have that walk around town and enjoy the river. Would love to get some photos of the bridges." John rubbed her back. "Check out some of those boutiques you like browsing."

"Hmm."

"We'll get a coffee somewhere nice and have a talk if you like."

"A coffee sounds good."

Constable McIntyre returned with his notepad. "You are staying at the caravan park in lot seventeen?"

"In Bluebell."

He glanced up with a question in his eyes.

"Bright blue caravan with white highlights. You won't miss her."

Now, he smiled. "Great name."

Daphne smiled back.

He checked the phone numbers for both of them were correct and shut his notepad. "Mrs Jones, your willingness to help is appreciated but please don't do your own investigation. One of us will be in touch." With a nod, he returned to his desk.

At the front door, John reached for the handle just as it burst open. Three people pushed past without as much as an excuse me, or sorry. They crowded into the area, forcing John and Daphne to squish up against the wall to avoid contact. John put an arm in front of Daphne.

"Where's the sergeant?" The speaker was a woman in her

late forties. She wore pink tracksuit pants, orange sheepskin boots, and a red sleeveless top, half tucked in. Her hair was a mix of grey and light brown and needed a good brush. "I demand to speak to him."

Two people were with her. A man about her age, balding, dressed in shorts and singlet with mud-caked leather boots. The other was an older teen and by his expression, he didn't want to be there.

Constable McIntyre returned to the counter. "Sorry Mrs Tanning, he's out."

"Out where? Why hasn't he arrested the serial killer?"

"Come on, love." John whispered and gently tugged Daphne's arm.

She pretended not to hear, her eyes on the scene at the counter.

"I'm not at liberty to say where."

She slammed her fists onto the top of the counter.

"That's quite enough, Mrs Tanning."

"No, you lot haven't done enough." That was the older man. "We want answers about our nephew's murder."

"We have no evidence of the cause of death as yet and—"

Mrs Tanning threw her head back and laughed. Everyone looked at her, including her husband and son. She stopped abruptly.

"Lisa Brooker married three men from one family over the course of five years and each one died within months of the wedding. Steve within hours."

Minutes, even.

"I am sorry for your loss. We are gathering information and will be in touch with any questions." The young constable's face had reddened but his manner was calm and steady. If the Tanning family were all like this, no wonder the police had their hands full.

The man spoke again, more under his breath than out loud. "Feud is killing us off."

"I'm not moving until someone in authority presents themselves to me." Mrs Tanning crossed her arms and leaned against the wall and her husband followed suit. The teen rolled his eyes and got his phone out.

John tugged a bit more on Daphne's arm and this time she let him lead her outside. A large flatbed Ute was parked half on the footpath and they went around it.

"Well, that was different." Daphne said. "Are we having a coffee?"

"You sound cheerful for someone who wanted to be back on the road in a couple of hours."

"There's something to be said for not being too hasty. I may have allowed my emotions to run away a bit."

John glanced at her. "So, we're staying?"

"Let's start with the coffee and see what happens."

WHAT HAPPENED WAS a text message that shocked them both.

Sitting outside in the morning sun was pleasant and they elected to sit in the fresh air with their coffees. The café they sat outside was small and quite crowded as people hurried in and out.

Daphne was in two minds about what to do thanks to the visit to the police station. It was clear how hard the small team was working to investigate Steve's death. If there was one thing she was familiar with, it was understaffed police stations. Back in their home town it was a one-officer set up. When Trev Sibbritt was the leading constable there, he'd managed. Just. Since he'd left to move to a new post in King-fisher Falls, there'd been a quick succession of appointees who'd decided not to stay. Hard work for one person when there's a large region to cover.

Little Bridges was bigger than River's End, but still a small town. It appeared they had four police officers in attendance which was probably sufficient for most situations.

"Doll? You are deep in thought."

Daphne smiled at John. "I was thinking about home."

"Anything in particular?"

"The police situation and how different it is from here. Lots more officers but my observation is they also have more trouble to contend with." Daphne picked up her cup. "Did you hear what Mr Tanning said under his breath?"

"Something about a feud."

"Yes. Feud is killing us off. I wonder…" she took a sip.

John leaned back in his chair with a small smile.

"What?" she asked.

"I can see your mind ticking over, Daph. But it isn't up to you to fix their problems."

"Oh, I wasn't considering that. Mrs Tanning is quite scary. But it does raise some questions about the history of the Brookers and Tannings. What is this family feud about? Are there more suspicious deaths on either side, I wonder."

"I would imagine the police have it under control, love."

He was right, of course.

Daphne gazed around as she sipped her delicious coffee. Many towns they'd stayed in recently had quiet Sundays with few or no shops open apart from the obligatory café or bakery. But Little Bridges was different. In either direction from where they sat, shops were open and people wandered. The atmosphere was almost festive and invited her to explore.

The strangest sensation gripped the back of Daphne's

head and the hairs rose on the back of her neck. Someone was watching her. She always knew.

With a casual movement, she let her eyes drift until she found the source.

It was the waiter.

Her heart skipped a beat.

Across and down the road, on the footpath, he stared at her.

Hoping he didn't know she'd seen him, she moved her eyes away. "John, don't be obvious about it, but if you look over my left shoulder to the other side of the road, can you see a young man?"

John took a moment to find him. "The one who is walking away?"

Daphne's head shot around. He had stalked off, glancing at her with a scowl before turning onto a path leading to one of the bridges.

"He's the one you saw coming out of the caterer's van? Possibly Lloyd?"

"He is. I could feel him staring at me."

"But why? If he's guilty of something, it doesn't make sense for him to draw attention to himself."

"Perhaps he wants to scare me."

"What?" John half-stood then dropped back in his seat. "Sorry. I think we need to finish our coffee, go back to Bluebell, and head to our next town."

The waiter's odd behaviour didn't frighten Daphne. It made her curious.

Her phone beeped as a text message arrived.

"Hold that thought, love."

Her eyes read the message but her brain didn't understand.

"Who is it?"

"Um…the mother of the bride of the wedding I'm officiating in two weeks. But why?"

"Can you read it to me?"

She would if she could find her voice. Her mouth was dry. She licked her lips, stumbling over the words. "Daphne, I'm letting you know we've decided to use another celebrant. Considering what is being reported on the news I prefer not to bring bad vibes to an otherwise positive day. Will send you some money to cover your expenses."

"Huh?" John sounded as confused as she felt.

Tears prickled at the back of her eyes but only for an instant. Her heart thumped an uncomfortable beat and she dropped the phone onto the table to clench her hands.

John scooped up the phone and read the message to himself, his forehead creased. "I don't understand. News has already travelled about Steve? And even so, what does his probably accidental death have to do with their wedding two hundred kilometres away?"

"Bad vibes."

"Doll, it isn't your fault."

"Do they think I pushed Steve into the pool?" her voice rose and a passer-by turned to look at her with a horrified expression. Daphne clamped her lips together.

"Come on. Let's go back to Bluebell and make some plans." John stood and offered his hand.

They walked arm in arm, following the direction the waiter took. When they were at the middle of the bridge, Daphne stopped. "I've made a decision, love. We're not going anywhere."

A MATTER OF WHO

John had to sprint to catch up with Daphne after her bombshell on the bridge. He'd frozen in surprise as his fired-up wife took off at a cracking pace towards the caravan park.

"Hang on a min, Daph!" he puffed as he reached her side. "Can't talk if...if you go so fast."

"Oh. Sorry, love." She slowed right down and slipped her arm through his. "Thought you were right behind me."

It took a minute to catch his breath. At least Daphne didn't look upset now about the text message. But what she'd just announced...

"Can you repeat what you said before you took off?"

She glanced at him with half a smile. "Which bit? That we have to stay in Little Bridges for a bit longer? Or the part about finding out what really happened to Steve Tanning?"

"The second part." He said. "You're serious."

"Of course I am. The poor police department is over-worked and it can't help them having the Tanning clan fronting up and wasting valuable time."

"But it's their job, Daphne, not yours. No matter how much your desire to help comes from a place of kindness."

Daphne stopped abruptly and turned to John. "I don't feel very kind. I've lost a client. What if I lose more?" Tears glistened in her eyes and John put his hands on her shoulders. "Being a celebrant means the world to me and all because of something happening which had nothing to do with my ceremony, I'm seen as...well, I don't know what. A bad omen?"

"Oh, doll." John dug around for a handkerchief as a tear rolled down her cheek. "Here, this is clean." He tapped at the tear and then wrapped Daphne's fingers around the cloth. "You are not a bad anything. There'll be a silver lining somewhere in there once you get past the shock."

"Lisa and Steve chose me. I promised them a perfect day and somebody stole that away from them. And from me."

"That's the point, love. Somebody else did this. Either by accident or design."

To his relief, she nodded. "You're right, John. But it hurts and from a practical, business perspective, I need to make sure my other clients understand how serious I am about my role in their important moments. They have to trust I will always put them first, even if I have to solve a murder to do so."

"Daphne?"

They continued on, following the path towards the camping ground.

"Daph, I know you have suspicions but what makes you believe the groom was murdered? You said he'd been drinking before and after the ceremony, so maybe he really did fall in."

"A definite maybe."

He had to grin. Her mind was ticking over and who was he to stand in her way? If there was one thing he knew about

Daphne Agatha Jones, it was that she didn't give up. Once she set her mind to something, she was going to get answers.

———

JOHN WAS the wisest person Daphne knew. And if he told her it was a mistake to pursue this new direction then she would listen.

Most likely.

There'd been the odd time in the recent past when she'd carried out her own investigations without his approval. Well, without his knowledge because that way he didn't have the chance to say no. Not that he'd ever try to boss her around. Their marriage was one of equality and true love. She'd seen his smile earlier and it warmed her heart.

"First things first." She announced as they climbed into Bluebell. "I think a pot of tea is in order and some more of those commercially prepared, overly sugary but somehow delicious biscuits of yours."

Daphne collected her large notebook, the one she used to scribble ideas for ceremonies. After finding a fresh page, she sat at the table while John made tea. "I'm going to write down everything I remember from the last two days. Every person I met or saw. All the incidents like people arguing and words spoken."

"Good idea. After our tea, do you mind if I do a spot of fishing? Let you have some quiet and I can find us something for dinner."

He needed some time to himself. Daphne understood. He'd want to process all the ups and downs of the past day or so.

"Sounds delicious! Well, once we cook what you catch."

She pushed the notebook away until they'd enjoyed their tea and gave John her full attention. By the time he changed into shorts and polo top and headed outside to collect his fishing gear, he was smiling and relaxed again. The way it should be.

You've got to be careful not to worry him, Daph.

Easier said than done, given how well he knew her.

An hour or so later, she stretched and got to her feet. She'd covered several pages of her notebook in writing and she'd clarified some things in her mind. What she needed to do was go back to the Brooker house and try to get some photos of the grounds. But how? She discarded the thought about sneaking around in the middle of the night. How would it look if she was caught? No, she needed a reason to visit them and then find a way to access the grounds.

A tap on the door interrupted her musings. "Forget your keys, love?" She swung the door open.

"G'day."

"Oh. Mr Brooker."

"Bertie. Nobody calls me mister anymore."

This was a surprise. Bertie stood a few feet back from the door, gazing at Bluebell. "She's a beauty. Did you fix her up yourself?"

Daphne climbed down. "We consulted on the work and I decorated inside. But we both were working full time so left the actual rebuild to professionals. Do you like caravans?"

"Used to build them. Had a big company. Once." He frowned. Moving closer to the side, he ran a hand over the join where a line of white cut through the blue. "Clever use of colour. Beautiful job."

This was a different Bertie from the one Daphne had met the last two times. The earlier disdain was gone, as was the sense that his mind was a long way away. Dementia was such a dreadful disease.

"Thank you. John and I are very happy with Bluebell... that's her name."

"And it suits her." He stepped back and crossed his arms. "Things aren't good at home."

"I'm very sorry for your loss."

His eyes didn't move and the longer he stared, the more Daphne got a sense he was sizing her up. She didn't think he meant any harm but his visit was unexpected.

"I didn't lose anything. But the place is like a mad house. Lisa weeping and throwing herself onto any comfortable surface whenever anyone looks her way. Bob and Margaret arguing all the time. House staff keeping out of the way."

"Grief affects everyone differently."

"Yeah. Hoping you'd come to the house."

"Me?"

"Say a few words. Don't celebrants do deaths as well?"

Daphne opened her mouth and closed it again as her mind raced. She'd wanted the chance to take photos. But the idea of another ceremony for those people had her blood pressure shooting for the stars.

"Nothing formal. Just the family gathered around. Thought Lisa might feel she has some closure. She likes ceremonies. All the pomp and glamour." He continued. "Not like a funeral. Just something to make her happy."

"Well, I guess I could."

"Good." He turned to go.

"But when? And I'd need some details."

"I'll talk to them. Want me to call you?"

"Please. Just give me enough notice."

Bertie waved as he walked away. He moved fast and with purpose in the direction of the river, but further north than where John fished. Daphne estimated the Brooker property backed onto it about two kilometres away. Bit of a hike for a man in his late seventies if her guess was right.

Back inside, Daphne added to her notes.

Under 'Lisa' she wrote:

Appears more upset when being watched.

Loves ceremonies.

The idea that Lisa killed Steve didn't sit right with Daphne. She might be a bit of an attention seeker but her shock at seeing her new husband dead was genuine. She was sure.

Beneath 'Bertie' she added:

Used to own a big company building caravans

Physically fit

The elderly man was at the bottom of her list of suspects but it paid to keep a record of her thoughts. One never really knew another person so how could anyone be above suspicion?

A FAMILY AT ODDS

Here she was, back at the Brooker residence as if it was two days ago. This afternoon there were fewer vehicles around, only a couple of cars in fact. The expansive front garden was empty of people and the place might have been deserted if not for Lisa's now-familiar raised voice coming from somewhere inside the house. Her words were muffled but her anger was clear.

Daphne sighed and glanced down the road. John was right at the end. Too late to turn back. He'd dropped her there after voicing his concerns.

"What if they treat you badly, love?"

"Bertie assured me everyone wants me there to discuss his idea."

"So, it isn't an actual ceremony yet."

Bertie had phoned just after John arrived back with a couple of fish in his bucket and a smile on his face. They'd had a nice salad for lunch before Daphne changed into tailored pants and a button up blouse. It would have to do until she could dry clean her jacket.

"No. Apparently Lisa wants to ask a few questions first."

Daphne had kissed John's cheek. "I'll be fine."

Once John turned the corner and the car disappeared from view, Daphne adjusted the strap of her handbag on her shoulder. If nothing else, she might get the opportunity to go into the back garden. Take a few secret photographs.

At the front door she knocked twice before footsteps approached. Rapid footsteps. The door swung open and a woman—tears streaking her face—hurried past, gripping a suitcase.

"Are you alright, dear?"

At the top step, the other woman stopped. "That terrible woman…how could she?"

"I don't understand."

"She wanted them all dead."

Other footsteps approached and the woman started down the steps.

"Wait." Daphne followed. "Lisa?"

"Margaret." The word was hissed and then, the woman was off again.

"Mrs Jones?"

Bob was again the person to greet her at the front door and as before, he wore a black suit. Perhaps he was an undertaker. Which would be useful with the amount of dead sons-in-law he had.

Daphne Jones! Too soon.

Afraid she might giggle from her nervous humour, Daphne kept her eyes down as she turned around.

"Are you alright?"

"Me?" she raised her head. "Um…yes, just admiring the mosaic tiles."

He screwed his face up. "Another one of Margaret's fancy ideas. Me, I'd be happier with a cabin in the woods. Please, come in."

All was quiet inside.

"I hope the cook didn't startle you."

"The cook? Oh. She was a bit upset."

"Happens all the time. This was because we got caterers in for the wedding."

A snippet of a memory popped into Daphne's mind. Walking past the kitchen where two women glared at her the other day. Yes, she'd seen her before.

"The others are outside on the deck." Bob led them outside.

Lisa, Margaret, and Bertie sat around a glass top table on a corner of the large deck in an area covered by clear roofing. A ceiling fan pumped warm air down, which didn't really help. Daphne was glad her jacket wasn't cleaned yet because even in the past hour, the temperature had risen.

Although it was early spring, this part of the country was considerably warmer than coastal towns. Little Bridges was surrounded by flat plains and known for its hot summers and cold winters. And now, as all eyes turned her way, at least one set were as icy as the season just gone.

"Daphne. Oh, I'm sorry..." Lisa burst into tears. She covered her face with what looked like a silk handkerchief and sobbed.

Bertie patted her back from the next seat. Bob pulled out a chair for Daphne and once she sat, he plonked himself down with a scowl, ignoring his daughter. Margaret smiled at Daphne. It was as forced and artificial smile as Daphne remembered seeing, and she'd seen a few over the years. And those cold, cold eyes of hers sent a short chill up Daphne's spine.

A young woman wearing an apron placed a tray with a jug of lemonade and glasses on the table and almost tripped over her own feet in her hurry to leave.

The sense of dread Daphne experienced leading up to the wedding was back in force. The Brookers were as dysfunctional a family as any in her experience. Mum and Dad at odds. Adult daughter who lived at home and lost her temper a lot. Grandfather on a decline but possibly manipulating them all. And staff frightened to do or say the wrong thing.

Why are you here, Daph?

Telling them to get counselling was an appealing idea. But leaving wasn't going to help uncover the killer. Assuming it was one of them. And now Margaret was top of the list thanks to the throwaway comment by the cook.

"I'm terribly sorry for your loss. All of you." Daphne began. "My heart goes out to you and Steve's friends and family."

Lisa dropped her handkerchief. Her eyes were suspiciously dry. "His family? Do you not know anything about them?"

Daphne shook her head.

"They are awful. Dreadful people who prey on others." Lisa glanced at Bertie. "Steal their hard work and dreams."

Interesting.

Bertie pulled a silver flask from a top pocket and took a swig.

"Dad, it isn't even mid-afternoon." Bob admonished.

"Isn't it? My bad." Bertie had another drink.

"My *bad*?" Margaret shook her head. "Really, Bertie. Time to stop being on the internet so much."

"Nothing else to do."

He exchanged a look with Lisa. A strange look which Daphne couldn't decipher.

Bob poured glasses of lemonade and passed them around. "We thought Dad's idea was a good one. Having a small ceremony to say goodbye to Steve."

"Except that is what a funeral is for." Margaret grabbed her glass.

"But Mum, we don't know when it will be. The police

said they won't have any news until at least tomorrow from the coroner and you must remember how long these things can take. I imagine Mrs Jones needs to leave sometime soon for her next appointment and then who will we get to say nice things about my husband. My...poor...husband." Lisa touched the handkerchief to her eyes.

Nobody in her family took any notice of her action but Daphne kept an eye on her. After a moment, Lisa dropped the fabric away and sniffed, then picked up her glass and drank. The silence dragged and only the distant mooing of cattle cut through the quiet.

"This is such a lovely spot you have. The house, gardens. How big is your property?"

Bob grinned. It was the first time Daphne had seen him look remotely happy.

"Almost a hundred hectares. Two hundred and fifty acres old school."

"I hear cows. Is that what you do here? Breed cattle?"

"We have half a dozen bovine grass mowers. And a couple of retired racehorses and a few sheep. Bit of a menagerie. No, we just like our space." Bob laughed.

"Besides," Margaret added. "We might live in the middle of nowhere, but showing the locals what a proper lifestyle is matters a great deal."

"It is a grand house." Daphne said.

"Isn't it? I had an award-winning architect come from the city to draw up plans."

"Good thing I love you, Mags. Spending all that money on the place."

"Well someone had to do something. Bertie would still be living in the last of his caravans near the river if I'd not intervened."

"Loved my caravan."

"It was a dump, Bertie. You were holding onto the past."

"Mum. How about facts?"

But Margaret had an audience and was on a roll.

"Mrs Jones doesn't understand what we've had to contend with. You see, Bertie once ran this town. Owned the biggest business and employed almost everyone. But he needed a partner and—"

"Mum! Stop it." Lisa stood so fast that her seat fell over. "Mrs Jones came to discuss a farewell ceremony, not hear about the worst of my husband's family."

"Isn't it three husbands?"

"Dad!"

With that, Lisa flounced away.

Bertie swigged from his flask, but he didn't seem bothered. If anything, he looked amused.

As interesting as these insights were, Daphne wanted to go after the younger woman and offer some comfort. Even if she was seeking attention with her exaggerated sighs and crocodile tears, losing her husband minutes after saying 'I do' was a dreadful tragedy. Daphne couldn't even imagine what she must be feeling. And she never wanted to know.

"Sorry about Lisa," Bob said. "She's an emotional girl at the best of times."

Margaret hadn't taken any notice of Lisa's exit. She'd sipped her lemonade and stared into the distance but when the conversation stopped, she glanced around the table, then to the chair on the ground.

"Tell us more about this farewell ceremony, Mrs Jones."

A HISTORY LESSON

"Did I mention what Bertie said about our Bluebell?" Daphne and John sat under the awning in twilight. Their dinner of grilled fish, potatoes baked in foil, and fresh bread rolls from the Little Bridges bakery, was now a delicious memory. John was doing far too much of the work, which did tend to happen around the times Daphne officiated ceremonies, but tonight a twinge of guilt reminded her it was time to give him a break. Tomorrow she'd manage all the meals and even find time to make cookies.

"What is that little smile for, love?" John leaned over and topped up her glass of apple cider.

"You look after me so well."

"Easy to do. Now we don't need to be involved in the day to day running of the real estate business, I am enjoying doing a bit for you."

John's original plan for retirement was to sell the business, but an offer from a young realtor changed his mind. Gavin wasn't in the position to buy but was managing the business with the view to buying in a few years. It suited Gavin. And them.

"And no, you didn't tell me what Bertie said."

"He said she's a beauty and the use of colour is good. He asked if we'd fixed her up ourselves."

John chuckled. "Much as I'd love to be that clever, it was a bit outside my skill set."

"You can turn your hand to anything."

It was pleasant sitting here as the sun set. The air carried the ruckus of native birds settling for the night, squabbling over perches and finding their spot. Little else moved close to their site. Only a handful of other caravans were in residence and none of them close by.

"You've not told me much about the meeting with the Brookers. Only up to the point of Lisa upturning her chair and leaving the conversation."

"She came back after a few minutes. Either she'd walked off her upset or…"

"Or?"

"I'm going to sound cynical and unkind. But it strikes me Lisa thrives on attention. Nobody followed her into the house."

"So the impact of storming off was quickly lost." John said.

"Her mother didn't even seem to notice Lisa had gone. She stared off in the distance the whole time. Oh. Not the distance." Daphne tapped her glass with her fingers. "It was at the pool."

"I would imagine that pool will give the whole family sad memories for a long time. How awful to have someone die on your property under such circumstances." John sighed and leaned back in his seat.

"I wonder where the others died?"

"Others?"

"Sam and Shane. Electrocution and falling off a ladder." Daphne reached behind her chair to a table beside the caravan and collected her notebook. "Might be worth finding out a few details of their respective demises." She scribbled some words. "Depending upon the coroner's findings about poor Steve, one would think Lisa would be a suspect."

"Love, don't you think you're speculating? For all you know, Sam and Shane might have had their accidents at work and anyway, they would have been investigated at the time."

Daphne grinned. "Which is why I need to find out!"

A magpie landed nearby and elegantly tiptoed towards the awning without a care in the world. The stately black and white bird stopped a few feet away and tilted his head.

"Feeding a baby?" John got to his feet and uncovered some uncooked fish pieces. He took one piece and tossed it close to the magpie, who wasted no time spearing it with a sharp beak before gliding away. "I heard a young one calling for food up in a tree near the river. Guess we're right in hatching time. I'll wash my hands and be right back."

As John disappeared into the caravan, Daphne added another note.

Why did Lisa choose three men from one family to marry?

It was a puzzle indeed. She gathered the Tannings were a large extended family but even so, Little Bridges wasn't so small that there wouldn't be other men to meet, let alone any further afield.

"Here I am."

"Where would you go to look for a husband?" Daphne said.

His eyes widened. "Sorry?"

She giggled. "If you were a woman living in a small community, where would potential husbands hang out? I never had to go looking, thanks to my high-school sweetheart." She smiled at John. "Market research."

With a slightly pained expression, John shook his head.

"I'm struggling with it. But what if we turn it around and ask where would a young man be likely to find a potential wife?"

"I'm all ears."

"My interest in genealogy might help us on this occasion."

"Oh. Research on marriages."

"Yes, along with other things. Some of the websites have interesting snippets about people's backgrounds, even where they met. Or where they were employed. So a shopkeeper might meet a customer. Church is a popular place for many reasons, not the least being the common ground of sharing a faith."

Daphne grabbed her pen. "Keep talking, love."

"A young man might be in a trade. A carpenter, possibly at a home to build an extension and meets the daughter of the house."

"An electrician who gets zapped at his new wife's house." Daphne was writing and only glanced up when there was no response. "Bad taste?"

"Daph."

"Sorry. Please keep going."

"Some things have changed over the years but people would still meet at school or college. They might work together." John said.

"What about socially?"

"Also shared interest in sports. Or hobbies."

After putting down her pen, Daphne swallowed some of the sweet apple cider as she thought about it. At the restaurant, they'd overheard the waiters say the Tanning boys were part of the cool set. Lisa came across as belonging to that crowd but would have left high school before Steve started.

"I wonder who Lisa went to school with? How would we find out when her previous husbands died? Or lived?"

"Best way to get a look at when they died is a quick walk

through a cemetery, assuming they were buried locally." John said.

Daphne clapped her hands, scaring away the magpie which had returned. "Oh, sorry, birdie. But you are so clever, John. Can we go now?"

"In the dark?" John shook his head. "You go. Not me."

"There's no such thing as ghosts."

"Still not going. Why not finish telling me about the meeting?"

He was right. She'd see more in daylight than with a flashlight in an unfamiliar graveyard. "The long and the short of it is they've asked me to do a farewell ceremony of sorts on Wednesday. Lisa is going to email some ideas across and Margaret will invite the bridal party to join the family. Keep it very small and quiet."

"Shall we plan on leaving on Wednesday afterwards? Gives us time for the drive to your next wedding location and to settle in."

"Excellent plan, love. As long as the coroner finds no evidence of a murder, there's no reason to believe we need to be here any longer."

HEARING AND SEEING STRANGE THINGS

Daphne finally got the chance to have a proper look at the shops in Little Bridges. John was content to go wherever she wanted. He didn't mind browsing with her, or waiting if she wanted to look at something he didn't find interesting. Which wasn't often as they had similar tastes and interests most of the time. Today they planned to be tourists. No talk of the wedding. Not even any writing up of the farewell ceremony.

While she was cooking breakfast for them earlier, Daphne announced it was time they enjoyed their visit to the area and forgot about everything else. She'd already spent an hour on the laptop checking her website. Thankfully no more cancellations but no new bookings either.

The first place they headed was the dry cleaners. Daphne handed over her jacket and pants with a smile and was promised it would be done by the next afternoon. Outside, he gazed around.

"Which way, love?" he asked.

"If you don't mind, I may need to buy another suit. With everything that happened...well it made me take a good look at my wardrobe. I have plenty of casual wear but not a lot for the ceremonies."

They spent the next hour or so visiting the half dozen ladies' boutiques. Daphne told John he didn't need to wait around for her but he was doing a bit of research on his phone and was happy enough to find a bench along the footpath.

John's interest in genealogy began years ago. Daphne came from a troubled background which he suspected was why she'd opened her heart and their home to foster children. And then, in midlife she'd found out about some discrepancies between her birth certificate and what she'd grown up believing.

Although she'd refused to look into startling revelations about her father, John made some quiet enquiries which led nowhere. There was no immediate family to consult. With the busy business they ran, he put it on the back burner and they'd rarely mentioned it since then. Now he had a little project of his own to make Daphne happy. He had no intention of telling her until sufficient facts came to light, and their current itinerary around Victoria was perfect for his research.

"Here I am!" Daphne sat beside him, both hands filled with clothing bags. "What are you up to?"

He slid the phone away. "Taking a look at a map of the area. I take it you found some clothes?"

"I've got two new jackets and then some pants which go with either." Then the other hand. "And some cooler tops seeing how warm the weather already is. I hope you don't mind."

John kissed her cheek and took all the bags. "Why would I ever mind? I love seeing you doing something nice for yourself, doll."

Their next stop was an ice cream shop. Cones in hand,

they crossed the road to the shade along the river. A long path meandered between the water and the main street, old trees offering respite from the growing heat of the day.

"What would you like to do next?" Daphne asked. "Didn't we see a fishing and tackle shop a bit further along?"

"I wouldn't mind a browse. I won't be long." Although Daphne enjoyed eating what he caught, she had zero interest in fishing.

"Take all the time you want and then come and find me in the bookshop over there once you're finished."

Sounded perfect. And a bookshop was about the safest place he could think of leaving Daphne on her own in this somewhat strange town.

———

STEPPING into the bookshop just off the main street in Little Bridges, Daphne sniffed the air to capture the unique and beloved smell of books. Delightful. Every wall was covered in bookcases and used books were piled up on the floor in the middle. Chaotic, but ideal for those who enjoyed rummaging. Behind a small desk covered with food wrappings, a woman in her thirties ignored Daphne as she tapped on a phone.

"Good morning!" Daphne smiled.

The younger woman grunted and didn't look up.

Well. You're a friendly soul. Not.

Customer service mattered to Daphne. She and John treated every person who stepped through the door of their real estate agency as a welcome visitor. When she visited shops and was ignored, she never knew if it was because the staff weren't trained properly, or that they weren't paid well, so didn't love what they did. Loving what you did mattered.

No point doing a job year in, year out, and not finding pleasure in it.

She pushed aside her feelings of being snubbed and browsed the shelves. There wasn't any order, with non-fiction sharing space with children's books. Gardening books with romance. Somehow, it made it more interesting. It took no time at all to lose track of the minutes. With carpet underfoot, there was hardly a sound as she selected a couple of mysteries to buy. When a phone rang, she jumped.

"Friendly Books. This is Tiffany."

The woman didn't even sound welcoming. Much less 'friendly'. Until she heard the voice on the other end and brightened up.

"I am so glad you called! Bored out of my head."

Perhaps talking to customers would help.

"Wednesday? Like, what time? And do I have to wear the stupid bridesmaid's dress?"

Daphne took a step back so she was out of direct sight of the woman but could see her through a gap in the bookshelves.

"No? Good. I know Lisa wanted yet another colour for this wedding but lilac did nothing for me. You looked good in it though." She listened and then giggled. "Next time we'll tell her we want black dresses. Perfect to wear at the wedding then straight to the funeral." She gave a shriek of laughter.

Hand over her mouth to stop herself speaking her mind, Daphne almost dropped the books. What a terrible thing to say. She peered at the woman and recognised her as one of the bridesmaids.

"Yeah, count me in. I'll tell the boss I'm sick. Probably enough leftover champagne at Lisa's to make it true anyway. Gotta go, babe, can see the boss heading in."

Off the phone, Tiffany threw the mess on the desk into a

bin and jumped to her feet, reaching a bookcase as the door swung open. An older woman with a walking stick shuffled in, muttered at Tiffany, and made her way to a door between bookcases which Daphne hadn't noticed.

"Bring me the orders book."

As Tiffany disappeared into the room with her boss, Daphne didn't waste a minute. Sending up a quick 'sorry' to the tidy bookstore gods, she shoved the paperbacks she'd chosen onto the nearest shelf and was outside before either woman returned.

"Whoa, Daph, slow down!"

She'd exited without looking and almost ran into John, who had both hands full between her shopping bags and a new fishing pole.

"Thank goodness it's you. We have to go."

Not waiting for a response, she hurried off.

"Daph, wrong way."

She needed to put a bit of distance between herself and Tiffany. Most likely she'd see her tomorrow at the ceremony and had no desire to be viewed as an eavesdropper. Again.

"Okay, we'll go the scenic route." John sounded amused from somewhere behind her.

At the next corner, she waited for him to catch up and for her to take a deep breath. There were less shops along here, apart from a large, modern supermarket beyond a carpark over the road. A white van was parked facing the street, its driver obscured by sun glare.

"Would you like to tell me what got under your skin?" John put the bags down to free a hand and put his arm around Daphne. "You ran out of the bookshop like you'd seen a ghost."

"Sorry. Accidentally overheard a disturbing conversation and didn't want anyone seeing me."

"What? Are you okay, love?"

A car drew up next to the van and when its driver climbed out, Daphne moved behind John. "Let me hide for a minute. She's less likely to recognise you."

"Who?" John followed the direction Daphne was looking in. "The woman?"

"It's Lisa."

Lisa was dressed in jeans and T-shirt, her hair in a ponytail and sunglasses covering her eyes. She went around her own car to stand at the driver's side of the van.

"Do you think they're talking?" Daphne whispered.

"Hard to tell from this distance. But why does it matter?"

"I know the van."

"Actually, now you mention it...looks a bit like the caterer's van. But, doll, it's a common brand. Lots of businesses use them and it isn't badged up."

"We need Charlotte Dean right now." Daphne said.

"Charlotte?"

"She takes photos of everything. What a good idea. I have my phone in my bag."

Doctor Charlotte Dean was a friend from River's End who'd moved to a new town where they'd recently visited so Daphne could perform a wedding ceremony.

"Do you think you should be taking photos of people without their permission? What if she sees you?" John asked.

"True. How about you take a photo. You're better at it."

John faced Daphne. "Neither of us are taking photos. Lisa is allowed to talk to people in her own town, and we aren't here to follow her around."

Over his shoulder, the van moved and Daphne peered around him. Lisa was getting back into her car and she raised a hand to wave as the van passed her.

"I wonder who the driver is?"

With an audible sigh, John picked up the bags. "I hear lunch calling. Time to go home before it gets too hot."

"Let me carry something." Daphne said.

"I've got everything but you are welcome to push the button on the traffic lights on the main street."

She giggled.

"Come on, young lady. You can tell me about the book-shop on the way home."

UNEXPECTED SUSPECT

John elected to have a shower to cool down when they reached Bluebell and Daphne was quick to take the opportunity to make some notes while events were fresh in her mind. By the time he emerged she'd put the notebook away and made lunch.

Determined to keep her earlier promise about staying away from anything to do with the Brookers, Daphne encouraged John to tell her about his new fishing rod and some accessories he'd bought. Most of it went over her head but his enthusiasm kept her interested. Then, she showed him her new clothes as she sorted them to wash or send to the dry cleaners in the next town.

"One can't be too careful with new things."

They decided to spend the afternoon playing board games. Outside, the sun was beating down in what was an uncharacteristically hot afternoon, according to John's internet search of temperature averages.

"Reckon there'll be a storm tonight." He opened the box of games they stored under a seat. "Getting a bit humid."

"You know, we've not had a storm since we've been travelling." Daphne poured glasses of icy water into glasses. "What if we're hit by lightning?"

"Not likely, love. Not with those tall gums all over the place."

"Oh my. What if one of them is hit by lightning and falls on top of Bluebell?"

"Think we're far enough away. Stop stressing before anything even happens."

Storms weren't Daphne's favourite event. And she should be well and truly accustomed to them after decades living in River's End. Being on the edge of the Great Southern Ocean, storms were common. She carried the glasses to the table, where John was setting up a game of scrabble.

"Good choice. You know you can't win."

"Fighting words!"

A tap on the door stopped the banter and John and Daphne glanced at each other.

"Mr and Mrs Jones? It is Constable McIntyre."

"My, oh, my." Daphne breathed. She slid out of her seat and opened the door. "Please, come in out of the heat."

The young constable took off his hat and climbed in. He was quite tall and seemed uncomfortable in the small space.

"Please, take a seat. Would you like some water?"

"That would be nice. Thank you." He perched on the edge of the spot she'd vacated. "I'm very sorry to intrude. Looks like you're getting ready for a game."

"You might have saved me." John said. "Daphne tends to win these ones."

"There you go. Iced water."

"Thanks. Mrs Jones, Mr Jones, I have some news."

"Please, it is Daphne and John, Constable."

"Matty. Call me Matty."

Daphne sat beside John, who moved across to make space.

"We received the coroner's initial report. It isn't complete yet. There's tox screening, bloodwork, all kinds of other findings yet to come. Anyway, without getting into the details, it would appear Steve Tanning was indeed murdered."

The hairs stood up on the back of Daphne's arms and her stomach clenched. She'd *known* it wasn't an accident.

"That is sad to hear. A young man at the beginning of his married life cut down like that." John said.

"The purpose of my visit is to ask you to come into the station and make a formal statement."

"Of course I will." Daphne asked, reaching under the counter for John's hand. "Are we allowed to know the cause of death?"

"Not at liberty to say. Not until further information comes to light." Matty drank the glass of water in a few gulps and set it down. "That hit the spot. Would now be convenient?"

"We'll drive over right away. Is it just Daphne you need to interview?"

Matty stood and opened the door. "At this stage, yes." He stepped down and gazed at the outdoor kitchen set up beneath the annexe. "Doing some fishing in the river?"

John joined him with Daphne close behind. "I am. Just purchased a new rod in town today."

On the side of the sink, the utensils John used for the fish were in a plastic container. Matty took a look and glanced at John.

"Mind if I borrow your filleting knife?" From his tone of voice, it wasn't a request, and he felt in his pocket and pulled out a glove.

"I guess so. Why?"

Matty lifted the knife by the tip of the handle and

inspected it. "Probably no reason. I'll get you to make a statement as well, Mr Jones."

Daphne had no intention of correcting the constable to 'call him John'. Her hackles were up. Why would the police have an interest in the filleting knife belonging to the husband of the celebrant from the wedding where a man was murdered?

Unless...

"Steve was killed with a knife." She crossed her arms and stared at Matty. "And you think we had something to do with it."

"I'D REALLY LIKE to know, please." Half an hour later, Daphne sat opposite a different police officer in the open plan station room. John was at another desk with Matty, his back to Daphne. It all reminded her of a bad television show from the last century.

Senior Constable Barber tapped on her keyboard for a minute before leaning back in her chair. "There's not a lot to tell."

"I understand you are waiting on more results from the coroner's office. And under normal circumstances—not that a murder at a wedding is normal—I wouldn't pry. But taking my husband's filleting knife for forensic profiling casts a different light on this. Do you believe he had anything to do with Steve's murder?"

As much as she was proud of how steady and calm her voice sounded, it was all a front for the panic coursing through Daphne. She wasn't good with uncertainty. Her hands twisted around each other in her lap.

"Assuming John wasn't present at the wedding as you've told us, then no, he isn't a person of interest."

"Then what? Do you think someone stole his knife, stabbed poor Steve, then returned it?"

The officer didn't respond but her eyes never left Daphne's face.

"Oh! You think I did it."

Nothing.

Unsure whether to laugh or cry, Daphne licked her lips as she considered her next words. The police might be guarded about the cause of Steve's death, but their action of confiscating a filleting knife gave it away. Somehow, it hadn't been obvious at the pool that he'd been stabbed but there'd been blood in the pool, on Steve and the man who'd helped. Even on her hands. She glanced at them.

"Care to comment?"

"Yes." Daphne lifted her chin. "I'm not a killer and I have no motive to murder a stranger, so let's get that out of the way first. What I can help you with is my observations of people and events from before the wedding right through until this morning. Some of which I have tried to tell Matty about in the past."

"Mrs Jones, isn't it true that Steve Tanning was rude to you the day prior to his death? That he was insulting in front of other people?"

"It is true. He said he thought I'd be younger. But if that was sufficient reason to harm him, why didn't I go after Bertie Brooker? He told me I was immoral for marrying Lisa and Steve. And then there's Gina, who is Lisa's great-aunt. She implied I am overweight, among other things."

Senior Constable Barber pulled her chair closer and rested her hands on the keyboard. Her expression had softened.

"What an unkind thing to say."

"It was. But the point I'm trying to make is that insults are never a reason to hurt someone. People say nasty things all the time and it is a reflection on them. Not the recipient."

With a nod, the officer typed a few lines, giving Daphne a chance to settle her racing heart. But John must be stressed about his interview. A sudden burst of laughter from him put that thought to bed. Her muscles relaxed.

"You said you have some observations to share. Where would you like to start?"

THE FALLOUT

Senior Constable Barber guided Daphne through the interview with no further mention of suspecting Daphne of wrong doing. Partway through, John joined her. The officer excused herself for a moment.

"Sounds as though you and Matty hit it off." Daphne said.

"He's a nice young man. Does a spot of fishing himself."

"Does he have a filleting knife?" Daphne muttered under her breath. She wasn't quite ready to be forgiving. John patted her hand.

The officer returned with some bottles of water and offered them to John and Daphne. "Warm day. Best to stay hydrated."

"Thank you." Daphne needed the water and drank quickly.

"So, we've covered the day before the wedding and the day of the wedding as far as the signing of the marriage certificate. Do you recall who else was there?"

"Lisa and Steve were seated in the middle of a long table otherwise filled with gifts. I stood to one side and their witnesses watched on. I have their names in my ceremonies book, sorry, I should have brought that along."

"We can check who they were."

"Some were from the bridal party. Not Tiffany though."

Senior Constable Barber tilted her head and Daphne explained.

"This morning I was in the bookshop and overheard a telephone conversation with the sales assistant. She answered the phone as Tiffany. And talked about being one of the bridesmaids."

"I know her. We'll come back to the telephone conversation shortly. What happened once the signing was completed?"

"There were photos taken as they signed and afterwards. Once I was no longer needed, I made my way to the house, but Mrs Brooker—Margaret—stopped me. She asked if I'd seen her father-in-law, Bertie." Daphne said.

Where was Bertie all that time?

"And had you seen him?"

Daphne shook her head. "Last I saw, he was walking in the opposite direction of the house. Margaret was worried he'd end up in the river based on previous incidents. She and Bob rounded up a search party."

"So the reception was delayed while people searched? It was quite an early wedding." Senior Constable Barber opened her own bottle of water and sipped.

"Apparently Lisa and Steve had a plane to catch that evening for their honeymoon and the reception was to wind down around six. But Lisa didn't search. She sat down with her bridesmaids." And a bottle of champagne. "Steve and his groomsmen followed Bob. Actually, Steve stopped to answer his phone."

"He had his phone on him?"

"A few things were different than most ceremonies I officiate for. But I'm there to marry folk, not judge their choices. The others all went ahead. I'm afraid I didn't see what Steve did."

"We can check who phoned and the time. Might help."

Daphne smiled to herself. Something she'd seen might be the key to finding the murderer. Who had phoned Steve? Surely it was someone asking him to go to the pool. The waiter?

"Mrs Jones?"

"Oh, sorry. Lost in thought. I got as far as the street when Lisa began to scream and I ran back to help. Steve was face down in the swimming pool. Bob and one of the waiters were in there, pushing him towards the side and then another man jumped in and between them, they turned him over." Her heart raced as she remembered. Poor Steve's vacant eyes. The blood on her hand. Lisa sobbing. "He was gone."

"Take a break if you like. This must be upsetting for you."

"I'm fine to keep going, Senior Constable. Finding the murderer is all that matters."

"Daphne was a strength to those around her." John chimed in. "She helped at the pool and then offered comfort to others. And from the start she believed it was a suspicious death."

"Why is that, Mrs Jones?"

So many people with something to gain. Or for revenge.

"Weddings are interesting events. At least for an outsider, like me. Many are filled with genuine love and happiness. Some also have an element of disapproval, or having some guests along who would be better left at home. But this wedding—or at least the time around it—had an adversarial feel."

"You've mentioned, to Matty and to me, some comments

directed towards you that weren't pleasant. I take it this isn't your normal experience?"

Daphne shook her head. "Far from it. I'm so lucky as a celebrant to be the one person most people treat well. Even at funerals. But it wasn't about how I was treated. Everyone was at each other, one way or another. Lisa was upset at her mother. Bertie was upset at everyone. Bob as well. Steve might have been one of those people who speaks without thinking or maybe he liked to stir the pot."

Matty wandered over. "Sorry to interrupt. Barbs, she's been picked up for questioning. They reckon they'll be here in twenty."

Barbs? Short for Barber. Nobody would call their child Barbara Barber. Unless she'd married a Barber. Stifling a giggle, Daphne realised everyone's eyes were on her. She was sensitive to being watched, much like this morning at the café.

"I just remembered something."

"About the wedding?"

"About this morning. The waiter was watching me from over the road while we had coffee."

"Which waiter?"

"Well, I did phone Matty about it… How fast can you type?"

"Sorry?"

"There's a lot to fill you in on."

AS THE INTERVIEW CONTINUED, John's eyes wandered around the station. Desks. A couple of whiteboards. Posters on walls, some for wanted criminals and others with motivational quotes. A small kitchen was through one door, a second one led outside, while another had a sign 'Interrogation and Cells'. Gave him a small shiver.

Daphne and the senior constable were in deep discussion. Matty had gone through the door to the cells and now emerged. Who was coming in? Assuming it was to do with the murder, was it Lisa or Margaret? What if one of the bridesmaids was a suspect Daphne hadn't pick up on?

He honed in on Daphne's words.

"I don't know the lady's name, but Bob referred to her as the cook. And she told me Margaret wants 'them' all dead."

"She left with a suitcase? Matty?"

Matty hurried over.

"Look into a staff member of the Brookers, please. The cook, perhaps. She left their employ yesterday in an upset state and may have some useful information."

"Yes, ma'am." He headed for his desk.

"Mrs Jones, you've been most co-operative. And there is a lot of information here so I'd like to go through it and then make up a report for you to sign. You mentioned you'll be staying until Wednesday afternoon?"

"Yes. Once I do the farewell ceremony, we're leaving for my next appointment."

"Lovely. Either Matty or I will be in touch before then."

Everyone stood and shook hands.

The back door opened and a police officer entered, followed by Lisa. A second officer closed the door as he came in behind them. Lisa's eyes were red and puffy as she glanced around.

The minute she spotted Daphne, she ran towards her. John instinctively moved to cut her off, as did the senior constable, but she got to Daphne first. And flung her arms around her.

"Daphne. Thank goodness you're here. Telling them the truth."

"Of course, dear. Telling the truth is all that matters." Daphne looked surprised, of course, but there was her genuine kindness shining through. She patted Lisa's back as she disentangled herself.

"They think," Lisa stopped, sobbed aloud, and put her hands over her eyes. "They think I killed my Steve."

"I would imagine these lovely officers are just getting statements from anyone involved. Witnesses."

"This isn't the first time I've been wrongly accused. But Dad will get our lawyer here and then they'll have to release me."

Behind her, Senior Constable Barber rolled her eyes, then nodded to the other officers. One stepped forward and gently took Lisa's arm.

"You're not under arrest, Ms Brooker—"

"Tanning! Mrs Tanning."

"Sorry, Mrs Tanning. Let's go have a chat and your father's lawyer is free to join us."

Lisa went with him, her sobs getting louder until she was out of sight and the door closed.

"Do you think she did it?" Daphne asked.

"Lisa is just one of several people of interest. And again, thanks for coming in and we'll be in touch."

John took Daphne's hand and nodded to Matty. They'd been dismissed and he, for one, was happy to leave this behind and step out into the sunshine.

A CHANCE MEETING

"Do you mind if we stop at the supermarket, John? In this heat, I'm thinking of taking some ice cream home." Daphne wiped her forehead. Clouds gathered in the far distance. "And some sedatives."

John laughed aloud and Daphne joined in. She'd never taken a sedative in her life but always joked about them when it was stormy. Laughing was every bit as therapeutic and by the time they reached the supermarket, some of the stress from the police station was gone. John parked not far from the door.

The air conditioning was ramped up high inside and Daphne considered staying there for a while. But there were only a few items to select and they lined up at the one open checkout. The sales assistant chatted to each customer at length and it took a few minutes until they were next. It didn't bother Daphne. Not when she'd had plenty of chats at the supermarket in River's End over the years. But the sales assistant interested her and she whispered to John. "Steve's aunt."

This time her hair was neat in a bun and she wore the supermarket uniform. But her voice carried as she regaled every customer with the sad news of Steve's death and the curse of Lisa Brooker. Either the customers weren't friends with the Brookers or they were too polite to say anything. With a bit of luck she wouldn't recognise Daphne or John, particularly as she'd barely glanced at them in the police station.

No such luck.

"You're that celebrant person." She crossed her arms and stared at Daphne.

John unpacked the basket without a word and from his body language, he was ready to intervene if it got nasty.

"I'm Daphne." Forcing a friendly smile, Daphne put her reusable bag on top of the shopping.

"A little bird told me you are doing something for those evil people. Some kind of ceremony."

Daphne was unsure how to respond. Her arrangement with the Brookers wasn't something she would talk about, at least, not with a person who made it clear they were enemies. Her heart sunk. Was Mrs Tanning about to do as Bertie did. Call her names. Or worse?

Dropping her arms, the other woman began scanning the shopping. "I'm Marlene. Steve meant the world to us all. His parents are inconsolable." She stopped and leaned across the counter. "Would you come and do a ceremony for us?"

"A ceremony?" Talk about unexpected. Daphne's mind worked overtime. This might be a gift of sorts. A chance to evaluate for herself if anyone from Steve's family might be responsible for his murder. "Of course."

John turned to her with his eyes wide. Daphne winked at him.

"Good. What about tonight?" Marlene said.

A gust of wind rattled the long glass windows.

"I need a little more notice. The best I can do is tomorrow." Daphne said.

Shopping scanned and packed, Marlene nodded. "Pretty sure everyone is around mid-morning. I start here at lunch time. Can I get your phone number to confirm?"

Daphne found a card in her handbag. "Email is best. Let me know the time and the address. Oh, and anything special you want said. And I will send you a return email with any questions and my fee."

A few minutes later Daphne and John were back in the car.

"Are you sure?" John turned the engine on. "All we know about the Tannings is what we've seen. People quick to anger and not afraid to get into a brawl."

"True, but there were extenuating circumstances, love. Fancy losing someone you love under such conditions."

"Even so."

"Let's see what the email says and make a decision then."

Daphne had already made her decision.

"I'm sure the Tanning family are nice people."

John's silence indicated he didn't share her optimism.

The sky was darkening as they drove towards Bluebell. Storm clouds loomed over the town, heavy with rain. The wind scattered small branches across the driveway.

"I might lock the awning down. Make sure nothing is loose in this weather." John pulled into their parking spot. "Let's get the shopping inside and I'll get started."

"And I'll help."

"You sure, love? Storm's close."

"Four hands will get it done faster."

As it was, they only just managed to pack the outdoor kitchen away, roll the awning into its travelling position, and secure the caravan before the first rain drops fell. John insisted Daphne go in as he did a final check and then, a minute after he joined her, a streak of lightning tore through the sky.

A STORY OF SUSPECTS

While Daphne busied herself making a pot of tea, John did a quick tour to make sure there were no leaks. The rain was heavy and relentless but Bluebell was rock solid. Not a sign of water where it shouldn't be. Daphne set their cups and the teapot on the table and sat, staring out of the window and jumping with every lightning strike.

"You're going to exhaust yourself doing that." John put her notebook and a pen on the table. "I know you have a million thoughts running through your mind, so what about you pretend I know nothing of this week's events?"

"You mean, tell you the story?"

"I was listening to you talk to the officer earlier and it had me thinking."

It was obvious John wanted to distract her from the storm, give her something else to consider. And he was the sweetest man because he must be bored silly with hearing about the murder.

"Thinking about what?"

"The cook. There has to be a story there. So why don't you run through your suspects—for want of a better word?"

She didn't need a second invitation. There was a lot she hadn't added to her notes. Daphne picked up her pen.

"Where shall I start?"

"Who and why?"

"I can do that." She flicked back through the pages and glanced at John with a smile. "There's a few of them."

"Perfect. We can pretend we're working on a game. Like Cluedo." He picked up the teapot. "I'll do this and you work through your list. Who is the chief suspect?"

Good question. It changed. And the more information that came out, the more often it changed. Much as her gut said the woman was innocent of murder, there was a stand out.

"The obvious one is Lisa."

"Why?"

"History. She married three men from one family group, all cousins. Each one is dead following what appeared to be an accident." Daphne made a note, reading aloud as she wrote. "Find out how Sam and Shane died. And how long the marriages were."

"Doesn't mean Lisa is responsible though."

"True. But she has a flair for the dramatic. As if any kind of attention is good attention. The wedding, for example. She made a big deal out of the wrong colour ribbons and carpet. And a lot of her crying produces nothing but big sobs. Now I sound cynical."

John put a cup near Daphne. "Not cynical. Looking with a critical eye. The way a detective would."

"Fair enough. In that case, I'm curious why she kept marrying Tannings." Daphne tapped her pen against her fingers. "The Brookers and Tannings appear to have some feud going on—Gina said as much the other night—so why would she bring the enemy of her family into their home?"

"Good point. Does she think it will stop the feud? Bring everyone closer? Or is it to rebel against her own family?"

Thunder boomed overhead and the rain intensified. Daphne's heart pitter-pattered faster and she bit her lip. It was just weather. She forced herself back to the notebook.

"I feel I'm missing something. There are a lot of odd connections and I can't work out where they lead. Not yet."

"If nothing else, you'll end up with a lot of stories to tell. You should write a memoir."

"Only if you take photos for me to include. Something else bothers me about Lisa—those close to her have little in the way of nice words to say. One example is her own father telling her she would never keep a husband." Daphne said.

"Which is coming true."

I wonder if he's making it come true. No, that's plain silly.

"Quite. Then there is her own bridesmaid joking about wearing black next time so they use the same dress for the funeral. The other strange comment was from Gina, Lisa's great-aunt. She asked me if Lisa had told me where the group was having dinner. Either Gina is paranoid, or Lisa has a history of bizarre behaviour."

"Or both."

He was right. The whole Brooker family might be a den of irrational fears and dark secrets.

Daphne started a new page and titled it 'Margaret'.

"She isn't high on my suspect radar, but Margaret has made the list."

John tried to hide a smile and Daphne kicked him gently under the table.

"More tea?" He asked.

"Thank you. And you don't have to sit with me, love. I'm really alright."

Before John could reply, thunder cracked overhead and the lights flicked off. Daphne squealed. Water poured down the outside of the windows in a sheet as if the sky had unleashed the ocean on them and the earlier heat of the day was well and truly gone.

The lights came back on.

"We have plenty of candles, doll, should the power go out."

"Sorry. Didn't mean to scream like that!" Time for this storm to be on its way. Daphne took a few deep breaths. "Actually, I take it back. I would like you to stay right here with me."

"I have no plans to be anywhere else. What if I take something from the freezer for tonight and we can have an early dinner."

It did sound good. At least if the storm continued, Daphne could cuddle under the blankets and hope the sound of the rain would send her to sleep.

MORE SUSPECTS

With the oven warming, John returned to the table. "On to Margaret."

"Yes. And she is of special interest."

"I'm curious, Daph. Lisa is in her thirties, married three times, but still lives with her parents?"

"I know. Unusual."

"Money? Security? But why if she's marrying someone? Wouldn't she move out?"

"Good questions. More to add to my future queries." Daphne scribbled the question down. "When I first met Margaret, I saw a mother who believed she was disappointing her daughter. She was crying and I thought it was because she couldn't please Lisa over the colour of the ribbons and so on. But what if she genuinely didn't want her daughter marrying Steve. She didn't like him."

"Because of how he spoke to people?" John asked.

"Probably didn't help. But I feel in my bones that something sinister happened between the two families in the past. She began to tell me about Bertie's caravan business and how he'd needed a partner, which was when Lisa stormed off. I have to wonder if this partner was a Tanning and it all went bad."

John opened his phone. "Happy to do a bit of research, love."

This was nice. The two of them working together to solve a terrible crime. Even if they were holed up inside with a savage storm rattling Bluebell's windows.

"The other thing about Margaret is her background. From what I've gathered, she moved from the city to marry Bob and was accustomed to a different lifestyle. Insisted on the design of the house being so—is ostentatious an unkind description?"

"With our lifetime in real estate we've seen every kind of home. But hers is out of keeping with the area and my first thought was if it is a way of showing off their wealth."

"Just going to the restroom. Be right back." As Daphne washed her hands a few minutes later, she stared in the mirror. Something was off about this whole family feud thing. She couldn't make sense of it yet, but it had to do with Bertie, and money, and him living in his old caravan by the river. "You'll figure it out, Daph. Let it simmer away."

"Think your phone just made the email arriving sound." John had got a piece of paper for himself and was copying information from his phone. "Anything else about Margaret?"

"Only the comment by the cook that Margaret wants everyone dead. Sounded as if it was straight out of the Lisa Brooker/Tanning book of how to dramatise events."

For a while, the only sound was the rain and thunder, as John wrote and Daphne read the email. From Marlene Tanning, it was surprisingly long and detailed, including a brief story to use about Steve as a child. Daphne found herself wiping a tear away. These people loved Steve and were no less entitled to a beautiful eulogy than the Brookers. More, if anything.

"Okay, love?"

"I'm going to write a lovely farewell ceremony for each family in the morning. For now though, we haven't discussed Bob yet."

"What makes him a suspect?" John put his phone down. "There's no big red flags around him that I've seen."

"No, just lots of little ones. He might very well have just been over the whole wedding thing, but Bob wasn't happy about having the event at the house. Said he'd rather have, and I quote, 'a cabin in the woods' than their mansion. Lisa annoyed him with her demands and even his father made him impatient." The hairs stood up on Daphne's arm and she held it up for John to see. "I have an odd feeling."

"About Bob?"

She shook her head. "Eyes on me. You know I can always tell."

"Not mine?"

"Never yours." Daphne slid closer to the window and peered through. "Surely nobody is out there."

John was on his feet and grabbed a torch. "I'll go and look."

"I'd rather you don't. You'll be drenched in seconds and all for a feeling. Which is gone now." Daphne stretched the muscles in her back, forcing the sensation away. It almost worked. "Too much thunder!"

After checking the door was locked, John sat again. "You sure? I can wear my wet weather gear and carry a fishing pole in a menacing fashion."

"Yes. But thank you." A giggle rose in her throat.

"Don't want you worrying."

"All this talk of murders. It was like when Bertie arrived. I was surprised to see him here."

"Speaking of Bertie, at least he can be omitted from your list." John stared through the window with his eyes narrowed.

"Negatory. I thought the same but despite his age and health concerns, Bertie Brooker is on the list. Aged he might be, but did you know he was once an elite athlete? A runner. His disappearance that day sent lots of guests on a wild goose chase and I, for one, have no idea where he was. Only that it gave somebody the opportunity to murder Steve without witnesses. If our speculation is right about bad blood over Bertie's business, then he might harbour a grudge strong enough to kill at least one Tanning. Or three."

John returned to his seat and lifted the piece of paper he'd been writing on. "I can shed a bit of light."

"All ears." Daphne said.

"I found an old newspaper article which I can't fully read, thanks to a paywall. But a visit to the local library might get the information. A decade or so ago there was a fight over Bertie's business and it did involve a Toby Tanning. Went to court but that is all I could access."

"Interesting. What if Bertie is killing off every Tanning who marries his granddaughter. For revenge?"

"Mustn't care about Lisa then." John said.

"Or cares more about revenge than about Lisa."

"Not a nice thought."

"Not at all. Mind you, if he does have dementia, as some of his family have suggested, how would he be able to plan and implement a murder which didn't even look like one?"

The next roll of thunder was further away. Overhead, the rain wasn't as insistent and no longer fell in sheets around Bluebell. John put their dinner in the oven. A casserole. Daphne tried to have a cooking day every fortnight where she'd prepare meals for freezing. They had chosen to allocate more than usual space for a combination fridge/freezer to make the most of fresh produce they came across in different areas. Soon they'd head towards Shepparton, known for its canneries where excess or second grade, but perfectly fine, fruit and vegetable products were heavily discounted.

"Earth to Daphne."

She laughed. "I can't wait for us to go to Shepparton."

John's expression of confusion made her laugh again.

"Sorry, love. For some reason, my mind was planning our future meals and I do love a bargain."

"And you can make the best meals from bargain purchases. I've watched you with a sense of pride and amazement over the years. And particularly when we had the kids."

A ridiculous tickle behind Daphne's eyes made her blink fast. Those were wonderful times, but hard times. The real estate agency wasn't always bringing in a lot of money and making sure every foster child was properly clothed and fed meant being creative. But Daphne grew up having to make do to get by and she used that to her advantage to create a better life for the wonderful youngsters who came into their lives.

As though he could read her mind, John reached across and squeezed her hand. "You did good. And look at us now with a blue caravan and the freedom to follow the road. I think there's a special bottle of sherry we've not opened, so I'm proposing a glass before dinner."

"I second your proposal."

John dug around in one of the cupboards and found a bottle and two glasses. "Think we were given this one by Christie and Martin."

Christie and Martin were dear friends living in River's End.

"I wonder what Christie would make of all this." Daphne tapped her notebook. "She'd most likely already have worked out who killed Steve, why they killed him, and where they are."

"You're not doing such a bad job, love." John returned to his seat and handed Daphne a glass filled with golden liqueur. "To solving crimes."

They clinked the glasses together.

"Last suspect and then dinner. It is beginning to smell quite delightful!" Daphne's tummy rumbled, which made a change from the thunder. "And although I said Lisa is top suspect, I really don't believe she is responsible. But this one…"

"The mysterious Lloyd."

"You read my mind. There is something about him which makes my skin crawl. The way he stares at me. And how he didn't respond when I apologised for almost running into him as he alighted from the catering van. Not so much as a smile. And the staring at the reception and near the café."

"It made you uncomfortable."

"Yes. It may be he simply doesn't deal with people well. But the damp shirt and fresh apron…something else is going on. I wonder if it was him in the van meeting Lisa this morning."

"And I'm curious about the interview at the police station. She was pretty upset when she arrived. It doesn't make sense why she would kill her own husband the very day of their wedding." John said. "They were about to go away on their honeymoon as well."

Daphne agreed. This town had something ominous going on—or at least, the Tanning and Brooker families did.

"What I just said about Christie—if we can work out the 'why', then the 'who' should be obvious. So why would someone kill a young man on the day of his wedding?"

AN ODD FIND AND A NEW PUZZLE

T he morning sky was crystal clear and the air was free of humidity as Daphne strolled along the river to work on her two ceremonies. She'd slept much better than expected and was woken by the enticing aroma of fresh coffee. Daphne slipped her feet into a pair of sensible shoes, shoved her phone in a pocket, and with her notebook in hand, gave John a quick kiss. He had his hands full putting the outdoor area back up.

There was a narrow track alongside the water and it made for easy walking, although the ground was still a bit soft underfoot. The river was higher than usual and swept fallen branches and other debris along in a hurry but otherwise there was little to remind her of the ferocity of the storm.

Talking to John last night about the death of Steve Tanning helped her mind focus on the facts rather than feelings.

"Although feelings matter."

She glanced around. Whew. Nobody overheard her. Not

even a squawk from the pair of magpies hunting for worms in the soft ground.

For a while Daphne dawdled along the track as she whispered ideas to herself. It wasn't only which words to use, but when and how to use them. Two grieving families. Two different approaches. Her intention with the Brookers was to tread lightly. As she already had a good idea of where each of them stood regarding Steve—unless one was the murderer—their ceremony offered some challenges. Best not to fuel Lisa's need for attention nor Margaret and Bob's dislike of the young man.

Daphne found a tree stump between the track and river and sat there to write her ideas down while fresh in her mind. For the Tannings, she formulated a celebration of Steve's life. Thanks to the email from Marlene, she had snippets to include. Writing about the good memories was easy. But how to broach what should have been the happiest day of his life without making it about the worst one?

"Can't really reminisce about how happy he was to marry his beautiful bride, only to end up face down in her pool."

She sighed and closed the notebook. His family hadn't even attended his wedding so mentioning it was bound to stir some distress. If they had been there, he might still be alive. Whoever was responsible for his death would have been forced to change their tactics with more people around. People who probably would not have joined the search for Bertie.

Daphne sat bolt upright. Was Steve's death planned, based on knowing his family wouldn't attend, or was it opportunistic? The answer to this question would narrow down the list of suspects. Presumably, the medical examiner would know the cause of death at some point, and speaking of points, if it was a knife then Matty must have information about the type of knife after his reaction to seeing John's filleting knife.

Weddings have knives. The cake knife—had anyone checked it? And caterers have knives.

Finding a blank page, Daphne noted her thoughts to come back to later. Perhaps she could pop around to the police station and see if there was any new information.

She got to her feet and her hands went straight to her behind. Damp, thanks to the soggy tree trunk.

"It rained all night, Daph. Now look at you!" Thank goodness there was nobody around to see her undignified wet bottom. She turned to go back but a movement across the river caught her eye.

Surrounded by thick bushes was an old caravan, perhaps a couple of hundred metres away. The only reason Daphne noticed was thanks to a person moving about near it. Her eyesight wasn't good enough to see much detail but she thought it to be a man. He wore a heavy, long jacket and hat pulled down over his head. In one hand he carried a bucket similar to the one John used for fishing and in the other, a short fishing rod. In a moment he was gone, behind the bushes.

How interesting. She scanned the area around the caravan. No sign of a car or other vehicle. No houses in sight. But this might be the back of the Brooker property in which case, the caravan would be the one Bertie once lived in.

Had it been Bertie? Hard to tell under the big coat and hat and the distance. If he lived in the house now, why would he bother with the caravan?

The alarm on her watch reminded her to get going. When she could see Bluebell in the distance, she took a short cut through the trees. And regretted it the minute she stepped into mud. Back on the grass she stopped to wipe the worst of the wet dirt off her shoes, glaring back at where she'd stood. By the look of the ground she wasn't the first person to misjudge the ground. There was another set of footprints. Much larger than hers.

How odd. Daphne took a closer look. The indentation was deep and faced Bluebell. Almost as if somebody stood here for a while. And just like that moment last night, the hairs stood up on the back of her arms.

JOHN DROPPED Daphne at the meet up point for the Tanning's farewell ceremony and nosed back onto the road. He'd been relieved it was at a park—rather than a home—just out of town in the opposite direction from the Brookers. When Marlene welcomed Daphne with a smile, the tension left his shoulders.

But after the chaos of the Brooker wedding…Shaking his head, John slowed the car.

Just up from the park was an old stone church, its wooden doors open. He found a parking spot under some trees and locked the car. Quite apart from how interesting he found country churches was the benefit of what usually accompanied them.

Sure enough, an old iron gate between overgrown hedges announced this was 'St Peters of Little Bridges Graveyard'.

The town's public cemetery was closer to the caravan park, the place for modern burials. Thanks to Daphne's celebrant status and his interest in genealogy, he often visited both public cemeteries and parish graveyards when staying in a new town. And seeing as he was going to wait for Daphne, he might as well use the time to indulge his hobby.

This graveyard was small and old with few fresh flowers and a lack of tending. Many of the headstones had crumbling corners and some inscriptions were hard to read.

"That belongs to one of the town's founders, Richard Brooker."

John jumped at the voice close behind.

"Sorry, son. Didn't mean to startle you." The speaker was a tall, elderly man wearing a dog collar. "I'm Father McIntyre."

They shook hands.

"I'm John Jones. McIntyre. Related to the young constable?"

"My late sister's grandson. A good boy."

"I hope it is alright for me to wander around? I'm a keen student of genealogy and I find beautiful small churches such as yours are often accompanied by local history."

"Spend as long as you wish. Is there a particular family of interest?"

With a gesture towards the headstone in front of them, John nodded. "You mentioned Richard Brooker as a town founder. What is his relationship to the current Brooker family?"

"Robert senior is his great-great-grandson. I think there are sufficient greats in there. Richard, from all accounts, was an upstanding man of faith. A hard worker who was fair in his business and private life."

"Robert senior is Bertie?"

"Yes. Bertie. And Robert junior is Bob Brooker." He led John to another headstone. "This belongs to Richard's one-time close friend and fellow town founder, Joseph Tanning."

"One-time?"

"Quite a history there. Do you have a few minutes?"

"My wife is at the park for a while so I'd love to hear anything about the families. What stopped their friendship?"

The priest glanced up at the sun and moved them both to a shadier spot. "Doctor says I have to reduce my time outside. Had some of those pesky skin growths removed."

"Not good."

"No. I rather love the sun, but there it is. Where was I?"

"The story of Richard and Joseph."

"Ah yes. Richard had several children in his middle years with his first wife before she sadly succumbed to a snake bite one summer. With youngsters to raise and his position in town requiring his full attention, he took a young woman on as a nanny. Before long, he'd married her."

"Giving his children stability again."

"Or so he thought." Father McIntyre said. "Joseph Tanning, who was almost the age of Richard, was also a widower and took a liking to the young lady."

Oh dear. John had a feeling he was about to be given shocking information.

"He enticed the new wife away from his friend and moved her into his...dwellings. Outrageous in any era but a terrible scandal back then. It was reported Richard flew into a rage, perhaps rightly so, and demanded her return. At gun point. A dreadful fight ensued and both men were mortally wounded. The wife disappeared, never to return. Within days, the Brooker children had no parents and the Tannings lost their patriarch."

A light breeze carried music from the direction of the park.

"Is your wife the visiting celebrant?"

"She is." John smiled. "At the moment she's helping the Tanning family with their recent loss."

"Difficult times. But a Tanning will never be anything to a Brooker than a thief. Sad, really." The priest gazed at John. "Are you interested in the graveyard for genealogy, or to help your wife find the killer?"

His surprise must have shown on his face for Father McIntyre burst into laughter and slapped John on the shoulder.

"You must remember who my great nephew is. He thinks highly of your Daphne."

And the young constable shouldn't be sharing confidential information, even with a priest. But John just smiled. "She was deeply shaken by the events at the wedding and wants to be certain the murderer is brought to justice. And she also knows the police have the investigation in hand, so would never intrude."

"Their resources are stretched. Always are when it comes to those families." Father McIntyre sighed heavily. "It has been a pleasure chatting but I have to close up the church and make my way to the back room at Bell's Bistro. Tuesday is bingo night and the older set—as well as some younger ones—will take me to task if I don't have everything ready."

He began to walk away then turned. "You and Daphne are most welcome to join us. If you care for a spot of bingo, of course."

"I'll ask Daphne. You've been most helpful, Father."

John got his phone out and spent a few minutes taking photos and writing notes. The details of these events were too important to forget. Events which just might still have an impact on the present.

ONE LESS SUSPECT

As Daphne and John drove away from the park, she dabbed her eyes. She'd only done a few ceremonies such as this one and the experience had proved more emotional for her than any of the funerals she'd officiated.

"The Tannings weren't like I expected, love."

"How so, Daph?"

"Despite their grief, every one of them thanked me for making Steve's last day a happy one. And for trying to help him at the end. As tough and blustery as Marlene came across at the police station, she is simply someone at the end of their tether and something of a spokesperson for the entire clan."

They passed the church, where a priest was locking the front doors.

"Father McIntyre." John said. "And before you ask, he is Matty's great uncle."

Of course John would have come to the graveyard. He did enjoy the history of these old towns and made friends so easily it was no wonder he'd chatted to the priest.

"Did you find anything interesting?" Daphne asked,

putting her handkerchief away as her emotions settled. Being back with her darling husband made everything right again.

"I did. But it can wait until we go out for dinner."

"Dinner?"

"Thought it time we visited Bell's Bistro."

Whatever have you been up to?

"Why do I get the sneaky suspicion this has something to do with the priest?"

"And the graveyard."

Daphne turned in her seat to take a better look at John. He glanced at her with a wink, then put his attention back onto the road.

"All will be revealed. Tell me about the ceremony."

Although she'd much rather find out what he was keeping for later, she knew John wasn't going to budge until he was ready to talk. He liked to think things through and be sure of his facts.

"Well, it was sad and sweet. Steve's parents said little. His poor mother barely let go of her husband's arm and both are clearly still in a state of shock. The rest of the guests were his extended family, of which there are many. Lots of cousins, aunts and uncles, two brothers. And friends, some I recognised from the bridal party. Someone bought a generator and they plugged in a screen with images of him and some videos from different ages."

"I heard some music."

"Yes. He played in a local band and they sang his favourite song. Everyone joined in which was kind of surreal."

"How so?"

Daphne smiled. "They're a heavy metal band so it was more like screaming rather than singing. But at the end of it, there was applause and hugging."

The car turned onto the main street of the town.

"John, would you mind stopping at the police station? I

just want to ask if they need anything else from us before we leave tomorrow."

"I'm sure they'd call."

"This might sound odd, but I'd rather know so I can stop thinking about it."

"Worrying about it, I imagine. Of course we can stop."

The police station was quiet, with only Senior Constable Barber present. "You are on my list of people to phone this afternoon, Mrs Jones. Couple of things to cross off if you have a few minutes?"

Daphne explained they only had another day here. "Just one more ceremony and then we have another wedding to attend some distance away."

"I have your report typed up if you'd like to sign it."

"Perfect."

The senior constable stepped away from the counter to collect the paperwork. "Sorry I haven't rung earlier."

"No trouble at all, but can I ask, if anything needs to be added, should I sign it now?"

"What might need to be added?"

Daphne shrugged. "With the Brooker farewell ceremony tomorrow there's always a chance I'd hear or observe something of potential interest."

"If so, we'll make a new report. But don't put yourself in a difficult position with them."

"I won't." Daphne signed where indicated. "Not likely to find me snooping around or peering through windows. But people do say things in front of me."

Senior Constable Barber made a copy of the report and gave it to Daphne. "You've been helpful and we appreciate your co-operation." She glanced around. "In case you were wondering about our interview with Lisa, seeing as you will be at her home again, we've excluded her as a person of interest. There are too many witnesses to all of her movements for her to have committed the murder."

"What if someone helped her?"

"We haven't ruled out an accomplice but can find no motive for Lisa to kill her new husband."

"Except a history of her husbands dying young."

"Not under suspicious circumstances though." Senior Constable Barber picked up her copy of the report. "Our enquiries are continuing and we'll have homicide detectives arriving to assist us in a few hours. As yet we haven't located a weapon nor been able to track the phone used to call Steve. That lead is one we are appreciative of, Mrs Jones."

They took her seriously. "So you think whoever phoned him was behind his death? Persuaded him to go to the pool and killed him there. Stabbed him in the back and pushed him in."

"Daphne." John put a hand on her arm. "Speculation."

"Not far from the truth though, Mr Jones. He wasn't stabbed in the back but it appears he was lured to the pool. But whether the caller was the killer is unknown. Thanks to accessing Steve's phone's SD card we know the number of the phone that called him. Finding it would help but the owner filed a report more than a week ago of its theft." The senior constable raised a hand as Daphne opened her mouth. "Before you ask, no, I am not at liberty to disclose the name of the owner." Little lines formed around her eyes as she smiled.

"Fair enough. Just one more question and I understand if it is off limits. I wondered if you knew where Bertie Brooker was when he wandered off?" Daphne asked.

"One of the staff found him not far from the house. He was sitting under a tree waiting for things to quieten down."

"Catering staff?"

"No. It was the Brookers' groundsman. Dempster. Before

you go, I'll fetch your knife." It was in a bag on her desk. "Matty, as a fisherman, should have excluded this on the spot. Too flexible."

John took it from her. "Appreciate having it back. Old favourite."

"Thanks again for your co-operation."

Outside, John took Daphne's hand and they returned to the car in silence. Once they both climbed in, he grinned at her.

"What?" she asked.

"Are you certain being a celebrant is the right choice? Back in River's End, Trev always talked about the fact Charlotte should join the police force and now I'm wondering if you also missed your calling."

She couldn't help but laugh at the idea of squeezing herself into a police uniform and wearing a badge. Much as Daphne respected those who kept the peace, it wasn't for her. More likely she'd make a good private detective. One of those old-fashioned ones with a hat and coat and magnifying glass.

"Does that sound okay?" John asked.

Daphne suddenly noticed they were back in traffic. "Does what sound okay?"

"Dinner about seven. Unless you have other plans."

"Nope. No plans other than dinner with my husband." She patted his leg. "And it is my treat because you've run me around all over the place this week." Best way to enjoy the extra money the Tannings had insisted she accept for the beautiful ceremony. "It feels nice to spoil you for once."

BELL'S BISTRO, BINGO, AND BAD WOMEN

It was just as well John booked ahead as the bistro was busy when they arrived a little before seven. Attached to one of several pubs in Little Bridges, Bell's Bistro was a large family friendly restaurant on two levels, plus outside tables. And it was noisy, but in a good way with conversation and music trying to outdo each other.

"I had no idea I was so hungry!" Daphne gazed around after they were shown to a table. It was a bit quieter here where a row of tables for two lined a long window. Up a couple of steps was a larger area with an indoor children's play area surrounded by bigger tables. The atmosphere was friendly and happy. "This was such a good choice, love."

"Although I did have an ulterior motive for suggesting it."

John still hadn't enlightened Daphne on why, nor shared even a word about his visit to the graveyard.

"You look very pretty. I like the new top." He said.

Even after all these years married, the sweet compliment made her smile. She reached out for John's hand and when he took hers, she held tight. "I love you very much."

"Are you ready to order drinks?" A voice interrupted. "Or shall I come back?

They released each other's hands. "What would you like, Daph?"

"You choose."

John asked for a bottle of local white wine and the young woman disappeared towards the bar. By the time she returned, they'd selected their meals. After ordering, John lifted his glass. "To discoveries."

"Oh. I like that. To discoveries!"

They clinked their glasses.

A waiter hurried past and Daphne craned her neck to see his face. Not Lloyd. If Lloyd was indeed the person from the wedding.

"I wonder if he does work here."

"Not sure he needs to be part of your list anymore." John said.

"But he acted suspiciously. And had a wet shirt. And stared at me."

"Yes. All of the above. But he might have spilled something on his shirt. And been surprised when you appeared out of nowhere. And looked at you wondering if you'd report him for being away from his post. There's always another point of view to consider."

True. He might not be guilty of anything other than being in the wrong place at the wrong time. And as far as she knew the police hadn't been interested in her information about him.

"Okay. Let's say he had no part in..." Daphne glanced around, not wanting to be overheard. "the situation. What makes you think he isn't?"

"Not sure at all. But you've been looking for a motive and I may have one which so far, nobody seems to have considered."

"You do?"

John told Daphne about his chat with the priest and the story of two men, once close friends, killing each other over the woman they both wanted.

"Let me make sure I understand. This was a young woman employed by Richard Brooker to look after his motherless children. And he married her. After a bit, his best friend decides he is prepared to destroy a lifetime of friendship by luring her away." Daphne said.

"Pretty much."

"What happened to her?"

"Disappeared. I'm planning on digging around a bit to see if there is any record of her after leaving the area." He picked up his glass. "Would you like to accompany me to the library in the morning and see if there are old records?"

"Maybe. Still need to finish the Brooker ceremony. But, love, what happened between those men was decades ago. Generations. Surely it would be forgotten and everyone moved on. Bertie even had a business relationship with one of the Tannings."

"Father McIntyre was specific about the feud. A Tanning will never be anything than a thief. That is how the Brookers view the Tannings." John said.

"I guess if Bertie and Toby also had a falling out, old feelings might have emerged. I wonder if Bertie would discuss it?" He'd been nice enough when he visited Bluebell. "Maybe I can speak with him away from the rest of his family."

"Not certain that's a good idea, doll. Dredging up a terrible history on top of Steve's death might upset him. What if we get onto the laptop after dinner and see what we can uncover?"

The arrival of entrees stopped the conversation for a while. This was their last night in Little Bridges and Daphne had mixed feelings about the town. Too many sad and distressing incidents came close to outweighing the good ones. Like now. Best to live in the moment instead of the past.

"This soup is delicious." John put his empty spoon into the bowl with a look of regret. "Do you find the food in small towns rivals anything in the city?"

"I do. Not that we've been to a city for…well, how long?"

Neither could put a year on it. Their life in River's End was busy and fulfilling so visits to Melbourne—the closest city but still several hours by road—were few and far between. There was a wedding coming up which would mean driving to the Mornington Peninsula and the best way was through Melbourne. And about the closest they'd get for a while.

At the end of the row where they sat, a glass door led to other parts of the building, including a room Daphne could see. Its door opened and closed regularly as people came and went, offering glimpses inside of long tables.

"Bingo night." The waitress cleared their bowls. "Popular with the oldies."

At that point, Gina and Pat passed the glass door and went into the room.

As soon as the waitress left, Daphne leaned closer to John. "I just saw Gina and Pat go in there."

He looked around.

"Into bingo?"

"I had got the feeling they didn't live here."

"What made you think that?" John topped up their wine glasses.

"At the other restaurant in the restroom, she said something about me not getting involved in her family's town. As in, their town opposed to hers. I took it that she was warning me off Bob and Margaret. Maybe also because she reminds me of Margaret, more than the Brookers. The way she dresses and speaks is more city than country and I assumed she'd travelled here for the wedding, if that makes any sense?"

John nodded. "It does. We're safe to believe she's Bertie's sister, given she referred to Lisa as her great-niece when she spoke to you. No doubt she is well aware of the Brooker and Tanning history."

Staring at the closed door to the bingo room, Daphne wished she was brave enough to go and ask Gina exactly what she'd meant the other night. But the woman had made it abundantly clear Daphne wasn't welcome. She'd even tried to quell the conversation around her table, telling the rest of the party a family feud was no reason to kill Steve.

"John!"

Her voice was louder than she'd planned but there was enough noise in the restaurant to stop anyone looking at her.

"Doll?"

"What if—and I'm assuming a lot here—what if the family feud is not the one about Bertie and Toby, but the old one. About Richard and Joseph? In which case, Gina and Bertie may very well have known their grandparents."

"And one of their grandparents would have been one of Richard's children!"

"Yes. What if the resentment towards the Tannings was so ingrained from a young age that Bertie made it his business to treat every Tanning as a thief?" Her mind raced. "But why would he then have one as a business partner?"

"Necessity. Didn't Margaret start to tell you he'd needed a partner?"

"Yes. I need to talk to Margaret. She might be a bit odd at times but she's the outsider, as it were and seems to want to chat to me. Do you really think I've been wrong all this time and the killer might be—"

"You're still in town."

Where did she come from?

Gina sneered at Daphne. She'd left her little black dress at home and wore satin pants and a blouse with a plunging neckline. Around her neck were more pearls. Different to those she wore the other night.

"We are." John stood. "I'm John Jones, Daphne's husband." He didn't extend his hand.

The waitress appeared with their mains and worked around Gina to put them on the table.

"When do you leave?" Gina eyed the plates.

"Would you like to join us for a chat? I can arrange another chair." Daphne offered with a wide smile.

"Why would I?"

"We're history buffs and it would be wonderful to get some local information from a member of one of the founding families."

"The. The founding family?"

"Of course. So I understand there was a falling out between the Brooker and Tanning families some time ago."

"Which is none of your business."

"True. But how interesting that three Tanning men have died and the connection, outside their relationship as cousins, is their choice of bride." Daphne said.

John hadn't moved and now, he crossed his arms, his eyes on Gina.

"More fool them." Gina said. "It would serve you well to stay out of our business."

"Are you threatening my wife?"

A sinister smile flickered across Gina's lips. "Take it as you wish. And Daphne? Why not order more potatoes? Or are you saving room for later?"

With that, the woman stalked away, almost running into a waiter who stopped dead in his tracks to avoid the collision.

John sat, his brow creased. "Daphne, what a dreadful person she is."

"She hasn't improved since we last spoke."

"Did you take her comment as threatening? I'm happy to call Matty."

Daphne's stomach churned. "Let's finish dinner and go home. It won't be long until we leave." But when Daphne lifted her fork, her appetite was gone. Mean words would do that to a person.

A MISSING KNIFE

John Jones was not a man to anger without good cause. Nor to wish harm on another. But he wouldn't have minded seeing Gina fall flat on her face. The warning shot was one thing, but to make it personal and bring Daphne's choice of meal into it was appalling. How dare she attempt to make Daphne feel bad with such a low blow. And it had hurt his wife. She'd finished her meal but without the normal enjoyment and critique of the food, and when he offered dessert she shook her head and asked to go home.

They walked back to the camping ground the same route as usual, stopping at the highest point of the bridge without a word. In comparison to the previous night, the sky was cloud-free. The river's level had dropped from this morning and it flowed slowly again, its dark surface reflecting the lights on either end of the bridge.

"This is such a nice town." Daphne turned her back on the river and leaned against the railing, her eyes on the shops peeking through the buffer of trees and bushes. "From a landscape perspective it is. I adore the old buildings and these bridges are worthy of their own picture book. Pity about the residents." Her voice was monotone and her face set.

"I'm so proud of you, love." John joined Daphne against the rail and put an arm around her shoulders. "The way you carry yourself, with dignity and kindness. It sets an example to those who use words to hurt and think so little of themselves that they seek to upset others." She didn't reply but her muscles relaxed and Daphne dropped her head onto John's shoulder. "When people resort to low blows it says a lot about them."

"I know. But I came here on invitation. To celebrate a wedding. There is no need for such rudeness." Daphne straightened and held a hand out to use her fingers to count on. "First was Steve. Saying he expected me to be younger. Then Bertie with his disapproval of my morals for officiating. And Gina. Not once, but twice she has sought me out to have a go at my weight."

"Nothing wrong with your weight. I love your curves."

Daphne kissed his cheek. "Anyway, I think she is just trying to be nasty any way she can. If it wasn't how I look it would be my profession. Or something else. Which leads me to ask if she is hiding something." She took one of John's hands. "I'd love another glass of the lovely sherry we had."

Good girl.

Nobody bounced back from a bad moment more than his Daphne. "Sherry and another search of the Bertie and Toby saga."

"Also, can you help me update my website? I have a few photos from the wedding. Unless you think it best not to include them?"

"Let's take a look first. And while we're at it, let's go over the ones you took in the caterer's van." All of a sudden, Daphne's hand slipped out of his as she picked up the pace.

"What a good idea! Coming?"

A sip of sherry was the perfect remedy for hurt feelings. Let Gina say what she would. Daphne had no intention of allowing the woman to get into her head again. She was probably perpetually cranky from being hungry.

"What would you like to do first, love?" John opened the laptop. "Shall I load your photos onto here and we can take a look on the bigger screen?"

While John did that, Daphne wrote down the latest information, thanks to his visit to the graveyard. "Just confirming it is Richard Brooker and Joseph Tanning?"

"Correct. I have images of the dates from the headstones on my phone."

Daphne found the photos in question and recorded the dates. This notebook was filling up fast.

"Here you go."

Daphne shuffled around to sit beside John as he clicked on each of her photos to make them fit the screen. There were quite a few from the signing.

"Margaret must have snapped away at anything. How strange to see Lisa and Steve together knowing it must be one of the last photos of him. Do you think I should offer these to Lisa...or even to the Tannings?"

"Might be a nice gesture. Did they open their wedding gifts even before the reception began?"

"Lisa unwrapped some before the wedding. Nobody thought to make a little table up for signing the wedding certificate so it was a last minute rearrangement to create a pretty spot. The flowers look really festive there."

John peered at the screen. "Are those steak knives?"

"Your eyesight is better than mine! I remember seeing a couple of knife sets and hoped the bride and groom weren't superstitious—not that many people believe it is bad luck these days, but still, not something I'd give."

"Maybe they'd be right to be concerned."

"Why?"

John zoomed in and then out a bit when it was too fuzzy. The steak knives were in a boxset, nestled in black silk.

"Is one missing?" Daphne asked.

"Think so. Now perhaps it fell out when space was being made. But look how pointed their ends are."

"Oh my. Almost as thin as your filleting knife!" Daphne fanned her face with her hand. "Have we just found the murder weapon?"

"Or where it came from."

"We should phone the police. Send the photo across so they can investigate."

John checked the time. "After nine. Not likely to be anyone there."

Daphne had already reached for her phone. "Can't hurt to try." She got Matty's card from her wallet and dialled. "If someone took the knife at the wedding, it might very well have been an act of opportunity. Oh darn. Voicemail." Daphne cleared her throat. "Good evening, this is Daphne Jones. John and I have some new information. About steak knives. Oh. At the wedding reception there were steak knives as a gift and one was missing. Anyway I have photos. Goodnight."

After hanging up she looked at John. He smiled. "Never know what to say to a machine."

"I'm wondering if I should dial triple zero."

"Emergency? That's for life threatening calls." John said.

"Well, what if the knife is used on someone else? Or thrown into the river? Actually, maybe that is what happened. Someone took the knife from the set, phoned Steve, met him at the pool and stabbed him. And pushed him in to make it look like an accident. Then they threw it into the river to avoid capture."

"Or the knife fell out on the table and is now safely back with the remaining set."

"John Jones, you are being far too sensible."

"Sorry."

She put a hand over his. "Sensible is good, love. But this is a murder and we have to think like a killer."

"We do?"

Daphne pulled her notebook closer and picked up her pen. "I'll draw the Brooker property. Here is the house." Her lines were angled. "Wrong shape but you get the drift. And the deck at the back and the pool off a bit to one side. This is where the garden splits in two."

She scribbled a row of x's.

"That's the hedge. On this side is where the wedding was held. And over here is the reception. You can't tell from my drawing but if you are in the wedding area you cannot see into the reception area. And vice versa. Hedges are too thick and high."

"Are you thinking someone took a knife during the wedding?" John said.

"If they did, it must be Lloyd or another of the catering staff. Everyone else was seated at the wedding."

"What about the cook?"

This was something Daphne hadn't considered. She nibbled on her bottom lip, playing with her pen.

John looked through the remainder of the wedding photos. "We need some from the actual wedding. Do you know who did the photography?"

Daphne shook her head. "There were a couple of people filming on their phones but Lisa said something to Steve about them not needing an official photographer. Going back to the cook...I saw her briefly with another woman in the kitchen. But that was the day before the wedding. Whether she was there on the day we'd need to find out. Bob said she was upset over them hiring a caterer so possibly she wasn't even on the property."

The phone rang. "That's the number I called Matty on." Daphne answered. "This is Daphne, may I put you on speaker as John is here?"

"Good evening, and yes, please do." It was Senior Constable Barber. "I just picked up the message you left. Can you elaborate?"

Daphne ran through the information about the knife set. "We were just discussing who might have had access. Do you know if the Brookers' cook was there that day?"

"Mrs Jones—"

"Daphne, please."

"Daphne. We appreciate you helping with this, but there's really no need for you to spend your time worrying about this case."

"Oh. Um, well it was just a passing thought. Because of the cook saying Margaret was trying to kill everyone."

There was a chuckle on the other end of the phone. John and Daphne exchanged a glance. "We've spoken to the person in question and she explained her comment. She's a woman who takes pride in her cooking and was offended by Margaret's insistence on using a caterer. In her opinion, they were likely to give the guests food poisoning which was on Margaret's head."

Plausible excuse.

"Good to rule her out then. But what about Lloyd? He was one of the waiters and acted strangely and—"

"Okay, okay. Just to give you peace of mind, we have taken a look at the van and there was nothing unusual."

"But I have a photo of his name badge on the wet apron."

"We have spoken to him as well as his team mates. He'd

spilled water on himself carrying a full tray of jugs and was seen doing so—in fact, some of the other staff made fun of him which he was upset about. All he did was throw off one apron and grab another and before you ask, we have sent the first apron to be tested for pool chemicals."

"What about the white tub in the corner?" Daphne pressed.

"Used for food scraps. Bit of a dead-end, I'm afraid. The detectives who I mentioned are here and running the investigation so while you are welcome to contact me with anything you think of, they'll be the ones to follow it up. Do you mind sending me a copy of the photo of the knife set?"

John leaned closer to the phone. "John here. Shall I send to the email on Matty's business card?"

"Yes. And thank you both."

The connection terminated.

"I'll send this now."

"Running out of suspects, love." Disappointment filled her voice. "Not Lloyd, although it doesn't explain him glaring at me those times. Too many people have alibis. Is it a sign that I should leave well enough alone?"

WORRIES AND PLANS

How was anyone meant to sleep with so many thoughts going on? Daphne willed herself to not toss and turn. John was out cold and needed his sleep, so why couldn't she relax and fall into the arms of slumber?

Counting backwards from one hundred was worth a try. One hundred, ninety nine, ninety eight...

Who is the killer?

There it was again, just as her mind drifted off. Worrying about it at night was pointless. If she imagined a golden beach with a hammock and a nice book…

And who did Lisa meet in the carpark?

This wasn't working. Daphne turned over, an inch at a time, sliding without pulling on the covers so not to disturb John. He mumbled and she froze. Pretending she was on a raft on a gentle sea, she squeezed her eyes shut.

Breathe in. And out.

What happened to the missing knife?

Bit by bit, Daphne slipped out of bed. Her dressing gown had fallen onto the floor and she grabbed it and her slippers. As quietly as she could, Daphne made her way to the tiny living area beyond the kitchen after collecting the laptop. If she sat facing the end of the caravan, the light from the laptop wouldn't reach John.

She checked her website. John had been busy after the phone call from Senior Constable Barber, cropping photos and uploading them with some captions. They'd decided not to include any with Lisa and Steve until the investigation and the funeral was over. As it was, Daphne was uneasy about sharing much about this particular wedding.

He'd done such a good job. There were three photos of Daphne. In two she appeared solemn and official but in the third she was laughing. Her eyes crinkled around the corners. There were a few images of floral arrangements, the cake, and the signing book open and laid across its pages, the beautiful pen Daphne provided for this purpose. All tasteful and appealing without giving away the bride and groom's identity.

She went back to the one of herself laughing. There'd been little to laugh at before, during, or after the ceremony and she couldn't recall the moment. John had imported all of her photos into a file so she opened it and searched for the uncropped image. Everyone in the photo was laughing. Steve was tickling Lisa and the pen had flown from her hand. Bob, the bridal party, and various guests in frame all laughed. But one face stood out with its grim expression. Daphne zoomed in.

Gina.

Daphne clamped both hands over her mouth.

She'd not noticed the woman on the day, which wasn't surprising given how many people attended the wedding. The creepiest part of this was not her lack of humour but the hatred in her eyes. Hatred directed at Steve.

One by one, Daphne inspected each photograph taken by

Margaret. Gina appeared in a few more but her attention was on something or someone further away.

Daphne attached the image of Gina to an email but even as she typed out the address to send it to the police, she changed her mind. How on earth could anyone consider the woman a suspect? Unkind, yes. Over-protective of her family, definitely. But in the photos she was dressed in a body-hugging cream dress, very high heels, and pearls. Not the attire of someone who would stab a man—one much taller than herself—then push them into the pool without a sound or becoming covered with their blood. And although not one to judge a person on appearance, Gina did not give the impression she'd have the physical strength to kill a fit young man.

Daphne yawned. Going around and around with the few clues available made her tired. She closed the laptop and tiptoed back to bed.

OF COURSE SHE OVERSLEPT, thanks to too little quality sleep. Daphne woke with a start to an empty caravan, reaching for her glasses to read the clock.

"Dandelions and ducks!" She swung her feet out of bed.

John had left a note on the table.

Gone to pick up brunch. Noticed you were awake in the night so let you sleep.

Daphne dashed into the shower. John was the sweetest man she'd ever met, but just this once she wished he'd woken her. With the Brooker ceremony this afternoon, she would be pushing it to finalise the words, and visit the bistro.

Or perhaps it was best to stop digging around. She turned off the water and grabbed a towel.

There were homicide detectives in town who had the

resources and knowledge to track down the killer. Daphne was—at most—an amateur sleuth. One with a keen mind and way of getting people to talk to her, but amateur, nonetheless. If she'd not been asked to perform the farewell ceremony today, she and John would already be at their next location. It wasn't her job or her place to uncover the face of a killer.

"Daphne, I'm letting you know we've decided to use another celebrant. Considering what is being reported on the news I prefer not to bring bad vibes to an otherwise positive day."

It was those words in a text message the other evening that set her on this path. Losing one client was awful. The bride and groom in question had already felt like friends yet they'd made the decision to cancel her appointment thanks to the murder of Steve Tanning.

"You could never bring bad vibes, Daph." She rubbed the mirror to clear the condensation. "They were scared."

But if more clients got scared and cancelled, not only would her budding career be over, but her heart broken. Before her eyes had the chance to mist over, she made herself a silent promise to be the best celebrant she could, including help solve the murder of one of her own clients. It was the only way she could prove her integrity. The only way she could stay proud of herself.

"I'm back, love." John's voice was a welcome interruption.

She stuck her head out of the bathroom door. "Morning! Be there in five."

It was closer to ten minutes later that she joined John and gave him a kiss on the cheek. "Take a seat and I'll bring coffee. There's savoury muffins and sweet croissants. Closest I could find for brunch to takeaway."

"Smells wonderful. And thanks for the sleep in. I was a bit restless last night."

John delivered two fresh coffees and sat opposite. "Too

much on your mind?"

Daphne gave him the short version of what she'd seen on the laptop and the thoughts bothering her the most.

"I agree, it is unlikely Gina was responsible for Steve's attack. Anyway, the police would have interviewed the family and if Gina had been missing for any length of time, it would have been noticed." John said.

"But what if she relies on her age and appearance of frailty to hide a lethal killing machine." Daphne nibbled on a muffin. "I wish I could work out who took Steve's life."

"Not a lot of time left, love. By the time you've finished with the Brookers, I'll have Bluebell all but ready to go. You'll have time to change for travel and then we can be on our way."

"Well, whatever I can't find out between now and leaving town, I'm sure I can continue to puzzle over." Or else she could simply get more clues before they drove away. "Are you still planning on going to the library?"

"I am. Care to join me?"

"There's still a bit to write for the ceremony but if I can get it done quickly I did have a thought. The local newspaper has its office not far from where we ate last night. I noticed it when we were coming back."

"You're thinking it might be worth dropping in there?"

"Never know what one might find in old papers. If you don't mind doing the library on your own, I might walk across and see what I can find."

With a quick glance at his watch, John nodded. "Four hours until you need to be at the Brookers. What if we meet back here for a quick lunch at one and then I'll take you there."

Daphne leaned over and kissed his lips. "I love the way you think. And then we'll be on our way again. Back on the open road."

148

A MAN NAMED MAURICE

It took Daphne less time than she'd expected to finish writing the ceremony. Her fingers flew over the paper and once she was happy, she transcribed the words into her ceremony book. This took longer as she was meticulous about writing neatly but when it was complete, she tucked the book into her briefcase and put on a pair of walking shoes.

Handbag over her shoulder, she locked Bluebell and donned a wide-brimmed hat to deflect the sun. It was a pleasant day without too much sting in the air. Perfect for a walk.

The route to town was familiar. Funny how fast one becomes accustomed to a place. She even knew where there were a couple of loose boards in the bridge over the river. From caravan to main street was ten minutes at a reasonable pace and Daphne didn't stop today at the high point of the bridge. Under any other circumstances this would be a town she'd spend more time exploring. Even returning to stay here again. But the upsetting memories would take a long time to fade.

"Enough of that." She muttered as she crossed the main street. There was only one purpose in her mind and a list of questions.

The 'Little Bridges Chronicle' was housed in a dark and narrow shop squeezed between a barber and a bank. Daphne had to peer through the window to be certain it was open, but the door was unlocked and she stepped inside.

It took a minute for her eyes to adjust to the dimness. A small counter was set a few feet back and beyond it were several desks. And not a soul in sight. Every wall was lined with framed copies of newspapers highlighting important headlines and interesting people. At the back, a rickety stair-case disappeared to another floor and beneath it was a room with a closed door.

It suddenly opened.

Daphne jumped. She'd thought nobody was in the building with her.

A man in his sixties, dressed exactly as Daphne imagined a newspaper boss would be—pants held up with suspenders over a striped shirt with the sleeves rolled up—emerged, a paper held in front of his eyes as he approached the counter. It was clear he had no idea she was there and when their eyes met, he uttered a swear word and dropped the paper.

"I am so sorry. Please forgive my dreadful language. I didn't know anyone was here." He swept the paper up off the floor.

"Don't apologise. I should have spoken."

"There's a bell on the counter." He looked. "Okay, there isn't a bell. I must find out where it is. Anyhow, I am Maurice." Hand extended, he smiled widely.

Daphne shook his hand. "Hello, Maurice. I'm Daphne Jones and I wondered if—"

"You are?"

I am...what?

"Mrs Jones, I am so happy to meet you. Please, please come and sit at my desk and I'll make you a coffee. Or tea? Or would you like water?"

"Water would be nice." She followed him to the desk at the very back. It was covered with files and so was the chair he gestured to before he disappeared into the back room again.

Despite the disorder, the feel in the room was welcoming.

"Oh dear. Here, you take the water and I," he grabbed the files from the chair, "will make space for you."

She sat with some amusement as he looked here and there and finally placed the files onto a neighbouring desk. Then he dropped into the chair opposite and smiled again.

"Now, where were we?"

"Is this your newspaper?"

"It is. I took over from my father almost half a century ago. He started The Chronicle after the previous paper slid into bankruptcy and I like to believe I honour his work." He waved a hand at the walls. "We've won awards for our reporting. Small, yes. But more than our share of articles have been picked up by national newspapers, even in recent years, which is incredible considering how much is online these days."

"Technology might advance us in many ways, but in my opinion, there is nothing like a real newspaper."

Maurice beamed.

What a lovely man. There was something so sweet and delightful about him. Perhaps his passion for the work that obviously filled his heart.

"So, Maurice, how do you know my name?"

"My dear Mrs Jones. Everyone in Little Bridges knows of you."

"Oh, my. I'm not sure if that is a good thing."

"I'd hoped to visit and ask for some comments from you

but as you can see," he gestured at the room, "no staff. All three of them off this week. Of all weeks."

Because who can plan ahead for a murder?

"Two of them are my son and his wife. How wonderful it is to see our family tradition continue and expand through marriage, but it takes two people away from the paper when they have a holiday. The third staff member went to Melbourne on Monday to be close to the coroner's court for any news and he's still down there."

"So...has he heard much?"

Tread softly, Daph.

"Pretty much what the police know, which I'm sure they've discussed with you." He leaned back in his seat. "Steve was stabbed in the neck and pushed into the pool, hitting his head on the way in. He was still alive but unconscious when he entered the water. Took next to no time for him to pass away. Darned shame for such a young man."

"You knew him. I imagine you must, having lived here for a long time."

"Know the family of course but Steve only from his sport and music. And occasional run-ins with the law. He's been mentioned a few times in The Chronicle for all three reasons." He laughed shortly. "Paper comes out Friday so hoping we get some leads to include."

"Leads?"

Maurice rummaged through the papers on his desk until he found a large notepad. "Keeping track of what I hear. Not that I'm about to do the work of our local police but I want our stories authentic. And as close to the source helps with that. So are you happy to answer some questions?"

"I am. But may I ask you some questions as well?"

Already turning to a new page, Maurice glanced up. "Ask, but whether I can answer depends on keeping confidentiality. Quite serious about protecting my sources."

"As you should. I'm curious about the arrangement between Bertie Brooker and Toby Tanning. The business arrangement."

As if to give himself time to think, Maurice inserted a perfectly pointed pencil into a sharpener.

Daphne continued. "The reason I ask is to get some context for a comment I overheard at a restaurant the night of the murder."

He stopped turning the pencil. "I'm listening."

Daphne smiled. "I may need to protect my sources."

With a big grin, Maurice tossed the notepad and pencil onto the desk. "We'll swap stories then. Bertie created a local caravan industry. Not only his business, which built them from the ground up, but complimentary businesses popped up. A parts manufacturer. A tourism shop based on places to camp. Even the caravan and camping park grew thanks to Bertie. But things changed over time. Bertie made some poor decisions and money was tight. Against Bob's advice, instead of retiring he went into partnership with Toby."

"I heard the families never got on."

Maurice waved his hand in the air dismissively. "A long time ago, perhaps. But generations change and although Bertie and Toby weren't close mates, they liked doing business together. All was well for a couple of years and then Bob started nosing around in the accounts—well, that's his job— and reckoned there'd been some...misappropriation of funds."

Bob was an accountant. Suited him.

"There were accusations and bad feelings and before you knew it, Toby wanted out which forced Bertie close to bankruptcy. Went to court. Got sorted, but after everyone was paid out, all that was left for Bertie was the land the Brookers now live on and a couple of caravans."

Daphne let out a breath she hadn't noticed she was holding. "How devastating for Bertie. I'm a bit confused though. Bob mentioned he had spent all his money on building the house."

"Bob's money?"

When Daphne nodded, Maurice threw back his head to laugh long and loudly. When he stopped, he found a tissue and wiped his eyes.

"Sorry. Did Bob really give you the idea he paid for the place?"

"He did. Was quite clear about the investment. Why?"

"The money came from Lisa. She had a huge inheritance when she was a kid. The second she turned eighteen she threw the money around like it was confetti and some landed with her mother, who had the house built. Bob was an onlooker."

The phone rang and Maurice apologised and answered, taking it with him for privacy.

This changed everything. If Lisa controlled the money then her reluctance to move out was understandable. As was her demanding behaviour. Bob and Margaret might live there but Lisa held the purse strings. It was time to take a closer look at Lisa's parents. Would they be fearful of losing their home and lifestyle when Lisa married?

"Apologies for the interruption. May I ask you some questions now?" Maurice asked.

"Of course, but about Lisa...who did she inherit the money from?"

"Her father when he died."

"Her...what?"

Maurice picked up his notepad. "Ah. I see that you thought Bob was her father. No. He's Margaret's second husband. And those ladies never let him forget it."

ANOTHER TWIST

I f it wasn't old graveyards, library reference rooms were right up there for John as enjoyable places to visit. Little Bridges Library was housed in an old, converted courthouse, complete with echoing hallways. Quite appropriate a setting for uncovering past crimes.

Seated in front of a microfiche reader loaded with copies of historical records from the region filled John with a sense of discovery. The librarian was most happy to assist, telling John few people even knew such devices existed today. She'd located records from the earliest days of the town and ensured he knew how to handle them properly. He did.

After setting the alarm on his watch to vibrate in one hour—knowing how he would lose track of time with research—he began his search. The records ranged from births, deaths, and marriages on public record, through to newspaper clippings. All the documents he'd requested focused on the two families who had shaped the early years of this town.

And still do.

Father McIntyre's story came to life as he read accounts

from a fledgling newspaper, Little Bridges Bugle. Richard Brooker was mayor of the town and owner of several businesses. Joseph Tanner ran livestock. Both contributed to building the town including the church John had visited. Joseph was a widower with one son when Richard's new wife took his eye.

The newspaper article was heavily slanted in favour of Richard, with the loss of his first wife mentioned several times along with his generosity to the young woman who was employed as a nanny but wanted her own family. Their marriage, according to the paper, was his way of giving her what she longed for.

It was less than six months later when she left Richard. There was a report of her disappearance being suspicious. And a week on, her appearance in town on the arm of Joseph. The next story was on the front page of the newspaper with the headline 'Scandalous woman destroys two families'. Images of a younger Richard and Joseph together in front of a timber and stone house. A rehash of the story of the death of Richard's first wife. And then inside, the account of the night Richard and Joseph shot each other.

John made notes from time to time. Daphne would be intrigued by this saga which continued for weeks with each story outdoing the previous in speculation of why and how this happened. Much was said about the orphaned Brooker children but only one mention of the Tanning boy, said to be living with his aunt.

Buried at the bottom of a long obituary for Richard was mention of his second wife. Mary Smith. "Had to be a common name!" Not one to let a small obstacle stop him, John finished up with the newspapers, and moved onto births, deaths, and marriages records. A glance at his watch gave him a hurry on.

The marriage of Mary and Richard was recorded but not another mention of her. Certainly not in this region.

His watch vibrated and with a sigh, John returned the microfiche to its box and turned off the reader. If he could ready Bluebell to leave early, then he'd drop Daphne at the Brookers and settle down with his favourite genealogy app. One never knew what might result from a good browse.

"I CANNOT WAIT to update you on everything I discovered!" Daphne had arrived back at Bluebell minutes before John and was readying lunch to put into a sandwich press. "Can you pass me the mustard?"

"Have a bit of news myself, but nothing which is going to change the direction of the investigation." He rummaged in the fridge. "There you are."

"Wish I'd visited Maurice earlier."

"Maurice?"

"Owns the newspaper."

"The Bugle?"

"No. That was the first newspaper. Maurice's father restarted it decades ago as The Chronicle. While I was there, he had a call from his reporter who is in Melbourne staying close to the coroner's office." Daphne closed the sandwich press. "Almost ready."

"Is there new information?"

"I have no idea how the reporter even found this out but apparently talk is that the steak knife idea has legs. The type of wound fitted a knife not unlike those in the photo. And the angle indicated whoever wielded the knife was a little taller than Steve."

"Rules out Gina, Bertie, Lisa, Margaret. Not Bob though." John collected plates. "How did the reporter find out?

Sounds like information the police would keep to themselves."

Daphne shrugged. "Not up to speed on procedures. And the paper isn't printing any of that yet. But Maurice asked me a lot of questions about the day."

"You were careful about what you said?"

"Yes, dear."

John smiled. "Sorry, doll."

"I was very careful. What you and I discuss is for our ears. But it didn't hurt to tell him about the wonderful nurse who worked so hard on Steve, or the paramedics who really did their best. He already knew something about a missing phone so I mentioned seeing Steve take the call. Can't see that it changes anything."

After lifting the golden toasted cheese sandwiches onto plates and slicing them, Daphne joined John at the table. "I've got enough time to do a quick read through of the ceremony and get changed."

"And I'll get Bluebell all but ready to travel while you do."

"Not once you drop me off?"

"To use your word? Negatory. I'll wait outside and do a spot of genealogy research. Leaving you alone with those people is not an option, Daphne."

She smiled. It was nice to be cared for so much. "I'm sure they will all behave. But it is good to know you won't be far if any of them show the slightest sign of being unkind. With a bit of luck, this farewell ceremony will go as smoothly as the Tannings' did."

Beneath the table, Daphne crossed her fingers.

SOMETHING TO HIDE

There were half a dozen cars parked in the driveway and along the street near the Brooker house. John kissed Daphne's cheek and promised to park where he could see her come out of the house, and made her promise to call or text him if she needed his help. She watched him drive fifty or so metres down the road, do a U-turn, and park beneath a tree. He flashed the headlights and she waved.

Rather than going through the house, Daphne followed the sound of soft music, which led her to the pool.

At the corner of the deck she abruptly halted, almost dropping her briefcase.

This was the last place she'd expected to hold a farewell ceremony, yet a small group was gathered inside the pool area. The fence itself was decorated with white lilies, white roses, and lilac ribbons. The music was from a string trio seated in the furthest corner. Hanging from the eaves of the change room was a long, white dress and Daphne gasped in recognition.

Lisa's wedding dress.

It swung back and forth, the mascara-stained top part of

the lace visible even from the distance. Daphne shuddered. What kind of macabre event was she walking into.

"Daphne!"

Lisa's squeal got everyone's attention and all heads turned as she rushed through the gate. Margaret, Bob, Bertie. The bridesmaids. The groomsmen. And two more. Pat and Gina.

Daphne's stomach turned. If that woman said one word…

"We've made it so beautiful for my Steve." Lisa slipped an arm through Daphne's. "We have music, flowers, champagne, and you. What could be a better way to farewell my husband than this?"

They went through the gate and Daphne stopped again. The pool was white. It looked as though milk had replaced water and she couldn't see the bottom.

"Isn't this nice? As if he is a ghost swimming around in there and when my wedding dress is lowered into the water, it will become one with it and him. And with your beautiful words to send him off, Steve will be smiling. Somewhere."

If Lisa wasn't holding onto her arm, Daphne would have turned and run. Heeled shoes and all. Her flight response was in full swing and it took several calming breaths to push down the panic. Margaret joined them, her face more solemn.

"Daphne, dear. Thank you for staying in town to do this. It means so much to our Lisa."

Daphne blinked. Words weren't coming but the other women didn't seem to notice. She found herself swept along to the same podium she'd stood upon only a few days ago. This was creepy.

Get a grip, Daph. It isn't about you.

Bob came forward to shake Daphne's hand. Released by Lisa, who returned to her bridesmaids, Daphne forced a smile. Not very successfully. Bob rolled his eyes as if to say he shared her sentiments. Or was he enjoying an inside joke only he knew? Another of his step-daughter's husbands out of the way. Revenge for forcing him into a lifestyle he detested, or a way to prove he held the upper hand—either were reasons a murderer might rationalise.

Nobody was above suspicion and only those with water-tight alibis were off the hook. Assuming they didn't have a partner in crime.

"Mrs Jones?"

She blinked. Bob had his hand on her shoulder.

"You look pale. Let's get you out of the sun for a few minutes."

About to say she was fine, Daphne clamped her lips together as he led her to the buildings. The change room door was wide open, as was the one opposite which housed the cleaning equipment. Bob pulled a chair from the change room and placed it against the wall between the two facing doors.

"I'll get you some water."

Bob disappeared towards the house and Daphne sank onto the seat. Everyone else was occupied and she leaned forward to better see inside the other room. No sign of the groundsman...Dempster? Shelves on the far wall stored all manner of cleaning products. A series of white tubs, one with the word 'Poison' on the side. Chlorine and other water treatments, cleaning equipment, lots of tins of paint. Perhaps he'd been the one who repainted the inside of the house before the wedding.

"Sorry, it's a bit messy in there."

Daphne almost fell off the chair. She touched her chest over the heart.

"Didn't mean to startle you." Carrying a long pole with a net on the end, Dempster stepped past. "Tend to keep the door closed so guests aren't put off by the chemicals and stuff but Lisa wanted access in case she decides to change the colour of the pool at the last minute."

After pushing herself to her feet, Daphne followed him in. "How would she do that?"

He leaned the pole in a corner and reached for a solid plastic container with a spout. "Pool dye. Well, it also has some other ingredients to make sure it stays opaque and it'll play havoc on the filters, but it does the job." Replacing it, he gestured to a row of smaller bottles. "Lisa initially wanted everything black but there was no way to make it happen in time. And not a lot of black flowers to match."

"And Lisa likes to match colours."

Dempster grinned. "She does. At least with white she's made everything look nice for the wake. I guess it is like a wake?"

Bob stuck his head through the door. "Got you a bottle of water. Demps, can you find Bertie?"

"Wasn't he just here?" Daphne followed Bob outside and accepted the chilled water. "Thanks for this."

"He'll be in the other garden. Probably thinks the cere-mony is there because the wedding was." Dempster jogged out of the gate, turning in the direction of the area through the hedge.

Bob muttered something about Bertie needing to go to an old folks' home.

"Once he's here, shall we start?" Daphne asked nobody and everybody. It was more a public service announcement to remind people there was a purpose for her presence. She opened her bag to get the ceremony book, readying herself to take centre stage on the podium when everyone was in place.

"Actually, I want to voice my objection to this entire circus."

Hand on the book, Daphne let it slide back into her bag as Gina stepped onto the podium as if she was the celebrant.

"The poor boy died in this pool." Gina pointed at it. "In there, Lisa. Yet you glorify this as though he was a prince instead of one of the thieving Tanning family."

"Now, Gina, let's not go there—" Margaret began.

"Go there? Should have gone there before the first wedding. Stopped the nonsense before it began. You should have raised your daughter better." Gina directed this at Margaret, who shrank back, almost stepping into the pool had Bob not steadied her. "And you should have stood up for your family. Your real family." This was to Bob.

A riot of angry voices broke out. Lisa burst into tears. What a surprise. The bridesmaids and groomsmen snuck off to a table near the string trio where champagne and glasses were set out for later. The music stopped.

Daphne stalked away, through the gate and up the path. Her heart pounded in her ears and if she didn't get away from this toxic situation she'd fall over in a faint. Just as Lisa had the other day. No. This was where she drew the line. This was enough.

A PARTING SHOT

"Should never have come back here." Daphne stomped her way towards the front of the house. The arguing continued behind her and she had no intention of ever looking at one of this particular family again. She'd find John and they could exit this town early.

"Daphne. Daphne, please wait!"

If that was Lisa following her then she could stop and go back to her quarrelling relatives.

"I might as well die as well!"

With a glance to the heavens, Daphne came to a halt.

"What does any of it matter? My husband is dead. All my husbands are dead. And I can't even say a proper goodbye because I have the worst family in the world." Lisa managed to add a sob at the end.

"I'm sorry, Lisa. I just can't be around this kind of nastiness anymore." Against her better judgement, Daphne turned around.

The sad figure in front of her tugged at something deep inside. It shouldn't, knowing many of Lisa's reactions were a performance, but there was a hollowness in the younger woman's eyes. No tears. No more sobs. But a deep sadness which might have been genuine. And there was something about the way Lisa wrapped her arms around herself which reminded Daphne of another woman. Much younger and long ago.

"Wouldn't it be best if you abandon the ceremony until people are prepared to respect your grief?" Daphne asked as gently as she could.

"But then you'll be gone."

Daphne crossed the distance between them and gave Lisa a hug. "I can leave my words for someone else to read. But I don't think I'm able to do this, not when people are yelling and pointing fingers. And your great-aunt Gina really doesn't like me."

"Gina dislikes everyone. Well, everyone who isn't a real Brooker. She never welcomed me. Or Mum." Lisa gazed back at the pool where a calm had fallen, at least for the moment. "Even though I made sure Granddad had a nice place to live and no more debt, his own sister reminds me constantly how outsiders took everything from him. But he thought Dad was wrong about Toby stealing from his company and it was all a misunderstanding, so when Sam asked me out on a date I figured marrying a Tanning man would help heal things."

Not the selfish person everyone painted her as. Not entirely.

Margaret was watching from near the gate. Her shoulders were slumped and all Daphne could do was take pity on the two of them. They weren't killers. Just outsiders trying to fit in with a difficult family whose past controlled their present.

"If you really want me to do this, let's go and do it."

"You mean it?" Lisa grabbed Daphne's hand. "I will never forget this."

Walking back to the pool with all eyes on her, Daphne had a feeling that she would also never forget today.

WITHOUT DOUBT this was the strangest ceremony Daphne had attended, either as a participant or celebrant. Nobody spoke, which was a relief, allowing Daphne to finish reading her prepared words, albeit faster than normal.

The milk-white swimming pool barely rippled as Lisa lowered her wedding gown into the water. It didn't sink immediately, but floated for a while creating a bizarre imprint on the surface. Everyone carried a wreath with white flowers and lilac ribbons and these were slipped into the pool as well. All the time, Daphne stood upon the podium clasping her book against her chest. And all the time, Gina's eyes bored into her.

When all the wreaths were in the pool and the dress was little more than a layer of lace and all of Daphne's words were done, the string trio began to play. In an odd turn of events, it was the same song Steve's band played at the Tanning ceremony although without the words, screaming, and tempo. The families had more in common than any of them would admit and it was sad they couldn't come together to share their grief and memories. At least Lisa had extended an olive branch. Several times.

Daphne dabbed her forehead with a handkerchief. The reflection from the tiles and pool accentuated the heat of the afternoon. Her bottle of water lay unopened on the chair she'd briefly used earlier so when the mourners drifted into small groups, Daphne abandoned the podium for the shaded alcove between the two buildings.

Both doors were closed. Dempster was outside the pool fencing as though keeping an eye on Bertie. The latter gave little away. He'd not got involved in the earlier argument as far as Daphne had seen. Did he even understand what was happening today?

"You can leave now."

Although her heart sank, Daphne didn't look at Gina as she returned her book to the briefcase. Was it even worth responding? If there was another crack about her weight or eating habits, there might be an unfortunate addition to the swimming pool. Almost made her smile.

"Take our money and go off to wherever you want to cause mayhem next."

"I believe Lisa is paying for the ceremony." Daphne straightened and removed the lid of the bottle to sip some water.

Gina opened her mouth but was cut off by Bertie's arrival. He pushed in front of his sister and put his hands on Daphne's shoulders, staring her straight in the eyes.

"You're a good woman, Mrs Jones. Thanks for helping Lisa say goodbye."

"That's very sweet of you to say."

"And a load of crock. Robert, why don't you do one of your famous disappearing acts? Your little helper over there can go with you."

Bertie winked at Daphne and released her. "Ignore Regina. She doesn't have a kind bone in her body and has a problem with anyone she's not related to and many she is."

Behind Bertie, Gina's eyes widened and her face turned a peculiar shade of red. This was about to become an ugly situation fast. Daphne collected her handbag and briefcase.

"If you'll excuse—"

"Perhaps you need to reconsider how you speak to me, big brother." Gina hissed. "Remember I know all the torrid secrets this family tries so hard to conceal."

With her back to the change room door, Daphne stepped sideways like a crab but Bertie closed the gap between his body and the corner of the building, his attention on his furious sibling. Then, Daphne aimed for a narrow opening around Gina but just as she moved forward, Gina put her hands on her hips, making it impossible to go around her without touching the woman.

Other people turned to look. Bob threw his hands in the air and walked off. One of the bridesmaids got a phone out and held it up as though videoing the pair. Being seen in the background was the last thing Daphne wanted so she opened the door to the maintenance room and stepped inside. She sent a text message to John.

Can you come around to the pool area? Might need an escort out.

Her phone went in her handbag, which she put on the floor so she could replace the lid back on the water bottle before it spurted all over her, thanks to shaky hands.

"The only thing you know is how to offend people." Bertie said.

More voices chimed in. Margaret. Lisa. Pat. Even Dempster, although all he did was ask them to both stop fighting which drew Gina's ire.

"How dare you speak to me! What are you? The groundsman. No, that overstates your purpose. You are a glorified cleaner and babysitter of an old man."

"At least Dempster cares enough to look for me. Like at the wedding. Nobody else came looking."

"Stop it!" Lisa forced her way between them. "Bertie, if you hadn't wandered off, Steve wouldn't have come to the pool. Gina, if you didn't make it so hard for his family, they would have been at the wedding and he would be alive now. You are both to blame and I'll never forgive either of you!"

Well, good for you. Tell them what you think, Lisa.

She did have some spirit after all.

There was a long silence and Daphne peeked around the doorframe. Gina still had her hands on her hips and her face was now as white as the swimming pool. Bertie grinned. He was enjoying this more than anyone should.

"I see." Gina lifted her chin. "Not that I need your forgiveness, Lisa. But you have all made it quite clear my contribution to this family is unwanted."

"Sure is, sis."

Gina leaned close to Bertie. Daphne had to strain to hear the words she spat.

"When the police come calling just remember you forced me to do it."

Bertie didn't flinch as Gina stormed away, out of the pool area and towards the front of the house. She passed John who was almost running in the opposite direction. He glanced at Gina and sped up. Daphne stepped out of the room. The way cleared around her as she ploughed through to meet her husband at the gate.

"Doll?" John panted.

"How about we go somewhere far, far away."

He put his arm around her and they turned their backs on the pool, the Brookers, the wedding dress sinking beneath the surface, and the dysfunction of the past few days.

BEGINNING OF THE END

"Dye in the swimming pool?"

"Yup. And her wedding dress, complete with mascara stains. Flowers. Wreaths. Oh my goodness, John. It was…different."

They were sitting in the car which was still parked under the tree. John took Daphne's hand and they looked at each other. Her lips quivered. How horrible this must have been for his wife. If this was the kind of experience to expect from her new career then perhaps it was time to reconsider it.

"Don't cry, love. It isn't worth it." He squeezed her hand.

"Wreaths with lilac ribbons. In a pool filled with dye which will wreck the filters."

"It's okay. You're safe." He almost held his breath. He should have gone with her. Insisted she have a helper, or something. How distressing this must be.

Then Daphne laughed. She closed her eyes and laughed until she cried, tears pouring down her cheeks. "The dress… it was like a horror movie…and Lisa said it would be…as though his ghost was there."

"Steve's ghost?"

"Yup. Her dress would be at one with him. And there was a lovely string trio playing Steve's favourite heavy metal song. And Dempster had to find Bertie again because he wandered off."

John found a small box of tissues in the centre console and handed them to Daphne. She took a few and wiped at her eyes. As much as she was laughing, he saw through it. There was pain there. And dismay that people would behave so badly.

"Let's get back to Bluebell." John started the motor. "Where was Gina going at such speed?"

Daphne didn't answer and he glanced across. She stared ahead, biting her bottom lip.

John pulled onto the road and accelerated.

"Gina was called out by her brother."

"Bertie? What did he say?" John asked.

"There was a lot of insults hurled between them and then Lisa told them both off. For once I actually liked her."

"Did Gina have another go at you?"

"She tried. But I was prepared and didn't let her get to me. Although I did consider pushing her in the pool at one point, but upsetting Lisa wouldn't have been worth it." Daphne leaned back in her seat. "I cannot wait until this town is in the rear vision mirror."

John agreed. He'd have them ready to go within half an hour. "Bluebell is almost ready. Get yourself into some comfortable travelling clothes and we'll be on our way."

Daphne reached over and patted his leg. "Thanks, love. You've been my rock through all of this and I'm so relieved we're not spending another night here." She settled in her seat again. "Sorry for all the emotion. I'm fine now."

If Daphne had needed to scream or cry he'd have understood. What a strong woman she was. John turned into the driveway of the camping grounds. A day or two away from here and both of them would be a lot happier. Nothing could stop that.

He backed the car ready to hook Bluebell up. Everything else was done. Awning and outdoor kitchen packed away. Power and water unplugged.

"Here we are, love." They climbed out. "Have you got your key?"

Daphne was ahead of him and she'd come to a halt. He thought it was to find her key until she turned with her hand over her mouth.

"What's up, Daph?"

She pointed back to Bluebell. The tyres were flat. Slashed, with visible cuts across them. They weren't going anywhere.

DAPHNE LOCKED herself in the bathroom.

She'd told John she'd gone to freshen up but she was there to cry. Except no tears would come.

This was her fault. The cost of replacing those tyres was more than she'd made for the two goodbye ceremonies which had kept them there. John wouldn't care, but he didn't need to be putting his hand in his pocket for something she'd made happen. If only she'd stayed out of it. Not nosed around and in such a way that other people noticed her interest. Other people who had things to hide and would stop at nothing to keep their secrets.

Secrets about families. About her family. Her parents kept secrets. Terrible lies.

Daphne's throat tightened and she gripped the sides of the sink, her eyes on the basin.

Yelling in the night. Words from behind closed doors which made no sense to ten-year-old Daphne as she cuddled her little sister to help her go back to sleep. Only years later did she understand what unfaithful meant. Let alone a much nastier word her father screamed at her mother.

Count your blessings, Daph.

She raised her eyes to the mirror. Those were memories. Not her life today. Not her life for a long time.

"You're a good person. You have a big heart." She whispered.

John loved her.

"A bad person slashed the tyres, Daph. Not you."

Eyes on her face, she forced herself to smile. Her muscles relaxed.

"You are perfect as you are."

Deep down she knew she didn't quite believe it. One day she would.

"Daphne Agnes Jones, you have a gift of seeing the truth and right now, there are people who need your help. Believe in yourself."

This time her smile was for real and endorphins flooded every inch of her body. Somebody had to solve this mystery and she might as well be the one to do it.

JOHN GOT OFF THE PHONE, frowning even more than when Daphne had found the tyres. "Not the news I'd hoped for, love. Nobody has four of the right tyres in stock in town. Best they can do is order them which means waiting until the morning."

"And there's no way to repair them?"

"None." He leaned down to run a hand over a gash. "Not a case of putting an inner tube in and patching the hole. These tyres are only suitable for the scrap heap."

A police car pulled up and Matty climbed out. "Thought you'd be well on your way by now."

"That was our intention. Thanks for coming to take a look." John shook Matty's hand. "These tyres didn't slash themselves."

Daphne left the men to inspect the damage and moved to the back of the caravan, her eyes on the trees near the river. Had the vandal waited there for them to leave earlier? This felt personal.

"Any idea who might be responsible? Noticed anyone hanging around?" Matty and John joined Daphne.

"Area is so quiet. Barely see any of the other campers let alone strangers." John said.

"Except somebody was watching us the other night." Daphne pointed at the trees. "From there, I think."

"What makes you say that?" Matty asked, holding his hand up to shade his eyes.

"During the storm the other night, I had the strongest sensation of being watched. And I know it was only a feeling, but when I was walking the next morning there were deep footprints around those trees."

John touched her arm. "You didn't tell me."

"Thought I was imagining things."

"What if we take a look?" Matty headed in the direction she'd indicated and the others followed, catching him up just before the trees, where he stopped. "Can you still see the imprints, Mrs Jones?"

I'll look silly if I can't.

Daphne was careful where she stepped as she circled the largest of the trees, glancing back to Bluebell. This was the spot. And the footprints?

"There. Just before the grass line. Facing our caravan."

Matty took out his phone and took a series of photos before getting close enough to inspect the area. "Looks like boots, large ones so most likely a man. And deep. Might have stood here for a bit. During the storm, you say?"

Daphne nodded. Someone had stood here watching them then returned and slashed their tyres. Quite apart from the cost of replacing the tyres was the knowledge someone wanted to harm them. She blinked rapidly and swallowed. No time for tears. Whoever the someone was, they were sending a message.

"At least you can rule out Gina!"

Both men turned to her with confused expressions.

"She has been telling me to leave town since Monday. Slashing our tyres means we have to stay longer."

Matty smiled. "We'll exclude Gina from our enquiries."

"But only for this. I just performed the farewell ceremony for Steve Tanning at the Brooker residence. Gina referred to his family as 'the thieving Tannings' and made a number of nasty comments of how other members of the family should have stopped Lisa marrying the three men. Her parting words to her brother were along the lines that he shouldn't be surprised if the police come calling and she'd been forced to do it." Daphne stared at Matty. "I wonder if she meant she'd felt forced to do something about Steve and had decided to confess."

Matty put his phone away. A long silence followed, broken only by birdsong. As if he'd made a decision, Matty nodded. "If Gina had anything to do with it, it was from a distance. She didn't stab Steve. Height is wrong and besides, she has an alibi. Everyone does."

"Everyone?" John asked. "What about Bertie when he disappeared?"

"Except he didn't disappear. He went to sit under a tree near the caravan waiting for Dempster to finish feeding stock or something. For some reason, the younger man can calm him when he gets worked up or confused. They came back together. And before you ask how we know, they were seen on the other side of the property at Steve's time of death."

Another suspect to cross off.

"Who saw them?"

"Shall we go back? I want to check for matching foot-prints around the caravan." Matty headed off without waiting.

Daphne hurried after him. "Please, may we know? It isn't like I'm going to go and accuse anyone!"

She was sure she saw a grin on Matty's face but he said nothing until they were back at Bluebell.

"Okay, it was Gina who saw them both. She was pretty angry about it because in her opinion Steve would still be alive if Bertie hadn't vanished and caused everyone to go searching."

"But she didn't want Lisa to marry Steve."

"A lot of people didn't but it doesn't make them murder-ers. You need to trust me that we've spoken to her at length about this and the missing phone and at this point, it is up to homicide to pursue any other angles."

"Missing phone? Was it Gina's phone that called Steve?"

Matty rolled his eyes and clamped his lips shut. It was fine with Daphne. He'd said enough to fill in some blanks. She couldn't wait to find her notebook.

NIGHT NOTES

"We finally have neighbours." John stuck his head through the door. "Apparently the people who were further up the river heard what happened and arranged to move closer. Strength in numbers."

"Were they concerned they might be next?"

"Nope. Didn't want us feeling alone."

Daphne shook flour off her hands. "What a lovely gesture. I should go and thank them."

"We will once they finish setting up. Thought I'd pop into town and pick up a bottle of wine to give them. Happy to wait until you can come with me."

"No, no. You go. I'm about to slide these cookies into the oven and thank goodness I've made a big batch so we can give some to those nice people. Do you mind if I give you a small shopping list? I fancy making lasagne for dinner."

A few minutes later the cookies were in the oven, John was on his way to town, and Daphne had her notebook on the table. After Matty left, John had climbed under Bluebell with a torch to make sure there was no damage he'd missed.

Four wrecked tyres was bad enough. Nothing else was out of place and some of John's expression of worry eased a bit.

Making cookies for him was the best way Daphne could think of helping. It was only a little thing but making something nice which he loved surely would provide some much needed comfort.

As the delectable smell of the baking filled Bluebell, Daphne added to her notes about the death of Steve Tanning. The police might have discarded Gina as a suspect but there were too many unanswered questions about her for Daphne's liking. For example, what did Gina mean about the police? Perhaps she had an idea of how to pin it all on someone else in the family. Like Bertie.

Daphne wrote down her thoughts until the oven timer buzzed. The cookies were choc chip and looked as good as they smelled. Perfect for a quick snack once John returned, before she started on dinner. Then, they could finally do a proper catch up on the events of the day.

AFTER DINNER, John did one final walk around outside, flashing his torch at the trees for good measure. Daphne closed the last of the blinds as he turned to come inside. The new neighbours were a couple of camp sites over and had their outside lights on as well. Best to keep everything illuminated overnight. Just in case.

"Matty said he'll arrange for the patrol car to drive through a couple of times tonight." John climbed inside and locked the door. "For all we know this might have been nothing more than a random act of vandalism."

Daphne disagreed.

"Would you like another cookie?"

"Um. Thanks but I'm still full. Dinner was delicious."

"In that case, I'd love to hear more about your visit to the library." Daphne dropped onto her seat.

John collected the laptop and his phone. "The library didn't give me a lot of new information but I was on one of the genealogy apps earlier, digging around to find Mary Brooker. Mary Smith. Let me go back to where I was because there were queries about her."

"So a person can join up and add their details to see if anyone is related to them?"

"Kind of. There are DNA tests people take—often just to get an idea of where their ancestors came from—and they can lead to discovering an arm of a family or a lost cousin. That kind of thing. Ah, here we go." John turned the screen so Daphne was able to see. "About twelve years ago there was a query about Mary Brooker of Little Bridges. An anonymous responder provided information including that she died in Melbourne aged sixty leaving behind a daughter. Well, well." He glanced up. "The child was born seven months after the deaths of Richard and Joseph."

"I wonder who the father was?"

"Excellent question."

"What if…" Daphne trailed off as she tried to connect her thoughts. "What if the query twelve years ago was from someone thinking they might be related to her, and therefore the Brookers. They find out about the Brooker wealth and come to claim their share. But the money is Lisa's inheritance from her father who wasn't a Brooker. She's only a Brooker because her mother has married into the family. So there would be no claim to stake."

"You think the Tanning deaths might be payback? Lisa didn't pay out so her husbands all get to die? Dunno. Seems extreme."

He was right. Sounded like a B-grade television show rather than real life.

"Here's another theory. This person descended from Joseph Tanning and came to join the family but was rejected. Actually, scrap that. Why only kill off those who marry Lisa?"

The lights flickered and Daphne jumped. John patted her hand. The lights settled and she told herself to get a grip.

"Right. Well, according to my notes, we are running out of suspects. Assuming we believe Matty that Gina is not one of them."

"Which you don't believe. Do you?" John stood. "Care for a glass of wine?"

"Great idea. I'd like to exclude the woman but really, how can I?" Daphne turned to the page headlined as 'Gina. Not a nice person'. "Let's recap as if you'd never met her or heard any of this and tell me what you think."

John poured two glasses of red wine and returned to the table. "Might be hard to pretend given how mean she's been to you, but let's give it a whirl."

They raised and tapped their glasses together with a 'cheers'.

Daphne put down the glass after a lovely long sip. "I do like the local wines here. Anyway, let me introduce you to Regina...don't know her married name. But a Brooker through and through."

"Nice to meet you, Regina."

"Funny. Although I'd like to mention that Gina takes herself very seriously, to the point of wearing pearls for any occasion and putting down other people to make herself feel better, I won't."

"Very charitable of you." John grinned.

"I thought so. Moving on to the facts as known. She is the younger sister of Robert Brooker, better known as Bertie, Dad, Granddad or Gramps. She has been known to say—on multiple occasions—that Steve Tanning didn't deserve to die."

"Which makes her a good person."

"On the other hand, she hates the Tanning family with a vengeance and has been overheard by a creditable source telling other members of her family they should have stopped any marriages between the clans."

"A creditable source. Well, that is reassuring."

Daphne giggled and drank some more wine.

"Why is this beacon of light even considered a suspect?" John asked, his eyes bright with mirth.

"Well," Daphne leaned a bit closer, "there are some things you may need to consider. Did you know she owns a phone which she claims was stolen before it was used to phone Steve on his wedding day? A phone call which lured him to his death?"

"Intriguing."

"Methinks she made herself sound sympathetic to Steve to draw attention away from her real purpose."

"Which is?"

Daphne leaned forward and whispered loudly, "Murder any of those thieving Tannings before they get another chance to steal."

John went back to the laptop, typing into the search bar. "Did you get more information about the deaths of Lisa's other husbands? Sam and Shane?"

"Some. Maurice from The Chronicle told me there had been investigations into both deaths but there was no evidence of foul play. Sam was an electrician working for himself. He was rewiring an old house and made a mistake. Was alone at the time and there was nothing to indicate anything other than a tragic accident. He was Lisa's first husband and they were together for seven months."

"Not long at all. And what about Shane?"

Daphne went back through her notes. "Fall from a high ladder. This was at the Brooker house and he was helping with a broken branch of a gum tree. Overbalanced and fell. Despite attempts to resuscitate he was pronounced dead at the scene. Married for three months."

"I'm on The Chronicle's website," John read from the computer screen. "This old article mentions Shane falling during an attempt by two men working alone to remove a dangerous branch. He was at the top of an eleven metre ladder with no safety gear and according to this, misjudged his footing and fell straight down."

"Nasty. And stupid. Why on earth take such a risk!" Daphne fanned her face with her hand. "Does it say who the other man was? Presumably, a professional tree lopper, although why they wouldn't bring their own people—"

"Love? The person with him was Dempster. And get this. His name is Dempster Smith."

"I CAN'T FIND my phone, John. It definitely isn't in the car?" Daphne turned her handbag upside down on the bed, lipstick, purse, and other small items spilling everywhere. But no phone.

"Even looked under all the seats and in the glove box. What is the last time you remember it in your hand?"

Daphne sat on the edge of the bed, concentration wrinkling her face. They'd spent the past ten minutes searching in the usual places. After the bombshell of finding Dempster's surname, she'd wanted to let the police know there might be a connection to Mary Smith and the original feud between the families.

"I sent you the text message. Yes, I'm certain I've not used it since."

"You were at the ceremony."

"I was in the room where they keep the cleaning stuff. I'd put my handbag down to replace the lid on my water. Then I sent the message and dropped the phone back into my bag. Except I was also listening to the argument so I must have missed my bag." She put her hand over her heart. "I have to get it back."

"We will, love. But not at night-time. Even if the family is still awake, it would be best to go there in daylight. And after speaking to the police. Don't you think?" John helped Daphne toss everything back in her handbag. "I'll give Matty a call now."

Daphne was quiet and followed John back to the table. He dialled the now-familiar number and got the voicemail. He kept half an eye on Daphne as he left a brief message and then hung up. He held his arms out and Daphne came straight in for a hug. Her heart raced against his chest and she was shaking. Wrapped up in his arms she gradually relaxed and dropped her head onto his shoulder with a sigh.

The phone rang.

"Sorry." John released her and kissed the tip of her nose before answering. "John here. Hello, Senior Constable, and thanks for calling back." He sat at the table and Daphne joined him as he outlined their latest information before disconnecting the call.

"What did she say?"

"Not to go to the Brookers tonight. Sorry, I know you want your phone back and we'll drive over first thing. She said she'll pass the information to the homicide detectives. She also said it is best if we stop nosing around." He smiled.

"We're not nosing around. We're contributing relevant details which the police may not have had access to. I can't imagine they have time to look at genealogy sites and why would they connect a dispute that happened a hundred or more years ago to a series of recent murders?" Daphne's voice broke a bit. "I think...I am pretty sure Dempster and Gina are behind the murders. All three murders."

A TRAGIC TWIST

The approach of dawn was a relief after a night which had passed slowly, with a head full of worries and fitful sleep. At least for Daphne, for John was a good sleeper and kept her thoughts company with his soft snoring. For once he wasn't up before her and she let him sleep until the sun lifted above the horizon. If she'd had her way, she'd have gone to collect her phone last night. It wasn't just not having it which upset her, but the knowledge a murderer might have found it. If she called her own number would Dempster answer?

Pushing aside the thought, Daphne put the kettle on then began opening the blinds. Everything outside appeared normal. The car looked fine, which was one of her overnight fears. Replacing four caravan tyres was bad enough.

"Morning, love." John disappeared into the bathroom.

By the time coffee was poured, he'd emerged and dressed. As he reached the table, his phone rang.

"Bit early." He peered at the number. "Don't recognise it."

"It looks like Lisa's number."

John tapped 'accept' and put the call onto speaker. "This is John Jones."

There was a long sobbing noise. Definitely Lisa.

Daphne and John exchanged a 'what now' glance.

"Is Daphne there?"

"I'm here, dear."

"Can you…can you both come here?"

"To the house?"

"Yes. And please hurry."

"Lisa, what's happened?" John asked.

More sobs, followed by a faint, "She's dead. Please come."

Then the connection ended.

"What on earth?" Daphne hurried to collect her handbag. "Margaret?"

"Or the cook? Don't even know if she came back."

"We have to go."

John gazed sadly at his coffee, but gathered his keys, wallet, and phone. "I guess we were going there anyway."

THE BLARING siren and flashing lights of a patrol car loomed behind them as John drove towards the Brooker house. It overtook in seconds.

"At least we know they've called for more help than just us." John said. "I'm not entirely happy about Lisa wanting you there."

"As you said before, we were coming here anyway. We'll see what happened, get my phone, and be out of here. What time are the tyres arriving?"

"Late morning and they'll give me a call before they bring them. Decent of them to fit them for me and to be honest, I was concerned I'd be trying to change them on my own." John parked a little way from the Brooker's driveway. "We might leave the car here in case it becomes hard to leave later."

On cue, another siren approached and as they got out of the car, Daphne and John turned to look. An ambulance.

"I'm wondering if we should go in, love." John watched the ambulance go into the driveway.

"If the authorities tell us to leave we will. But Lisa sounded distraught. And my phone."

As they walked to the house, people emerged from other homes and came to their front gates, all heads towards the Brooker property. With every step, the sense of déjà vu intensified. Another day, another dead body. What else would be repeated? Bertie disappearing? Gina having another go at her?

"Once I have my phone I am never leaving it anywhere ever again." Daphne muttered.

Police and paramedics crowded through the front door. Lisa appeared from the side of the house and frantically gestured for Daphne and John to come to her. Once they reached her, she hugged them both like long lost friends.

"We have to hurry."

She took off and they followed her past the house, deck and pool. Then through the gate to where the wedding had been held.

"Lisa, you didn't say who died. What happened?" Daphne puffed as she half-ran to keep up the cracking pace Lisa had set. John grabbed her arm to help her along. Not that he was breathing quietly either.

"The most dreadful thing has happened."

There were voices not far behind and Lisa sped up, skirting behind the still-erected backdrop from the wedding and through a space between more hedges. Daphne scraped her arm going through but what she saw on the other side made her forget it on the spot.

This was a large paddock with a few sheep huddled at its far end beneath some trees. Past them the caravan sat by the river.

Face down in the middle of the paddock was a woman. Her body fitting dress and pearls were a giveaway before Daphne was close enough to see her face which was turned in their direction with her eyes closed. A steak knife was in her back.

"My, oh my. Gina?"

"Yes. Didn't I say that on the phone?"

"No. Lisa, we shouldn't be here." John stopped a few metres away and held Daphne's hand to stop her going further. "Careful where you step, doll. Evidence and all that."

He was right. But Lisa was kneeling beside Gina. "This must be the same knife that killed my Steve. It came from the set we were given for our wedding and one was missing, but you know that because the police said they saw one of your photos."

"Lisa, you should step away. What if you accidentally destroy evidence?"

"Too late, Daphne. I found her here when I was going to check the sheep. They were carrying on and now I know why. After she stormed off yesterday we didn't see her again. Pat phoned last night to see if we knew where she was."

The police and paramedics made their way through the hedge, lifting the stretcher through. Bob was followed by Margaret and Bertie. The latter pushed past and ran towards Gina's body. Lisa leaped up and met him partway.

"Don't look, Granddad. She's gone."

"No. No, not my sister." He skirted around Lisa and dropped to his knees near Gina. "Not my sister. What has he done?"

"Bertie? What has who done?" Daphne asked.

He shook his head as though he didn't understand, his hands wringing each other.

"You said what has he done? Can you tell me who 'he' is?"

The police were closing in and Bertie glanced at them, his mouth opening and closing before he managed, "The killer. That's who. It's gone too far."

In a moment, the area was swamped by police and the paramedics. Daphne took John's hand and tugged. They retreated to the hedge and watched from there as paramedics declared Gina was gone. The officers were ones they'd seen at the station but not spoken with. Bertie was on his feet with Bob supporting him.

"Bertie knows something." Daphne said.

"Got that feeling. Do you think he suspected Gina was behind Steve's death? That she got on the wrong side of whoever she was working with?"

"Let's get my phone before the police stop anyone moving about."

They were almost at the pool when Lisa chased them down. "You can't leave yet!"

"My phone is in the maintenance room. I accidentally left it there yesterday."

Lisa sprinted ahead and was unlocking the door when they reached her. "That's why your number went to voice-mail. I hope it's still there."

So do I!

Door open, Daphne hurried in. The phone was on the floor. She swept it up, checking it but the battery was flat. "Thank goodness. And thank you, Lisa. But why did you need us here?" She gripped the phone against her chest.

"They'll think it was me." Her voice was steady as she gazed at Daphne. "After the things Gina said yesterday about Steve, I'll be blamed. At least until they do their forensics tests and find I'm innocent. Somebody has to find the real killer, Daphne."

Her mind already turning over possibilities, Daphne was confident Lisa was not involved in any of the deaths. Which left just a handful of known suspects.

"Lisa, where's Dempster? I wonder if he heard something from the caravan."

"No idea. But he comes and goes as he pleases as long as he does his job. I phoned him when the sheep were carrying on earlier and he didn't pick up. And now I know why the sheep were upset."

"Should we get the police to check the caravan?" Daphne zipped her phone inside her handbag. No more risk taking.

"He's probably sleeping off one of his nights of binge drinking." Lisa relocked the door after Daphne exited. "Gina was nasty to him yesterday and it doesn't take much to send him on a bender. That's why he never finished his medical degree. Too stressful."

Medical training?

Outside the pool fence, Lisa stopped and ran a hand over her eyes. "Once this is all over, I think I'm done."

"Done, how?" Daphne asked.

"I've tried to fit into this family but nothing works out. I don't remember much about my real father but he left me a lot of money and it made a difference to Mum having the kind of home she had always wanted. And gave Bertie a safe place instead of slumming it in the old caravan. But nobody is grateful. And I've lost three husbands thanks to a family feud my mother married into."

One of the police officers emerged through the gate between the hedges, glancing around and spotting the three talking. He spoke into his radio and began walking towards them.

"I'll head him off so you two can leave. And thanks for

everything, Daphne. Maybe one day when I live a long way from here I'll get married again and give you a call to do the ceremony." With that, Lisa straightened her shoulders and made a beeline for the police officer.

"If the police need to speak to us, they know how to find us." John looped his arm around Daphne's waist. "Best we make sure we're back at Bluebell when the tyres arrive."

Daphne couldn't help looking back. Lisa and the police officer had disappeared and only the still-milky coloured swimming pool indicated anything unusual had ever taken place here. Two murders. A family as dysfunctional as Daphne had ever met. And a mystery still unsolved.

DAPHNE'S DECISION

John had rarely been so happy to pull up near Bluebell. All he needed was four tyres and a helping hand to replace those damaged ones and they'd be on their way out of Little Bridges. No more murders. No more difficult and even nasty people. No more worrying when the phone rang. Back on the road with his wife and the wind at their back.

"I feel I should have stayed."

Surely he'd misheard her? John climbed out of the car. "Might put the kettle on before the tyres arrive. For that matter, we didn't get to have breakfast."

Over the roof of the car, Daphne gave him a puzzled look.

"Need to eat before we head off on the next adventure." He said.

"We've not quite finished this one."

"This, my bride, is not an adventure." John locked the car. "Nightmare, yes. And one we need to escape from before the next instalment drops into our laps."

Daphne followed him into the caravan. He started the coffee while she plugged her phone in, giving him little glances from time to time. Going back to running a real estate agency held a certain appeal at this moment. He'd seen two dead bodies in the space of a few days and now Daphne wanted to go back to where they'd been. Where one still was.

Two arms encircled his waist as Daphne suddenly hugged him. She must need some emotional support after this morning. And he could do that. He could look after her and make sure nothing bad ever happened…John gulped.

"Shh. It's okay, love. We'll get through this." Daphne whispered as she squeezed him. "Not nice seeing Gina, was it? But we are outsiders and can be helpful and that makes me feel useful."

He held on to her until he could trust himself to speak. Whatever had come over him was back under control. The kettle boiled and he gave her a quick kiss on her lips as her arms dropped to let him go.

"What would you like to eat?" she asked.

"Cookies."

"For breakfast?"

John grinned. "Why not. Coffee and cookies. Not like it is early now. More like morning tea."

Even though Daphne raised her eyebrows, she was quick to collect the container storing the rest of the cookies from yesterday and leave it open on the table. He brought the cups across and they sat.

"Why do you think you should have stayed, love?"

"Oh. I thought you hadn't heard me say that, but it occurred to me somebody needs to keep an eye on Bertie."

"An eye?"

"He might be distraught about his sister, but what if he does suspect who the killer is and confronts him?"

John knew he'd regret asking but did so. "Confronts him? Which 'him' is the killer?"

Daphne helped herself to a cookie and nibbled on it for a

minute. Her expression was thoughtful and John waited patiently. All of a sudden her eyes met his and his heart sank before she spoke.

"Do you mind showing me something on the genealogy site?"

"Just leave me here and go back to Bluebell."

"Nope. If you are going to insist on this then you're stuck with me."

They stood at the front door of the Brooker house. Neither had knocked because this debate had gone on for the past three minutes. It was surprising nobody had come to the door to demand an explanation for their presence. Daphne had changed into her new pants and jacket. A professional look made a difference. At least to her confidence because it wasn't helping her stay cool. She stepped further into the shade.

She'd put the pieces together and the best opportunity to test her theory was back where it all began. But John was getting more and more concerned and she was second guessing the wisdom of dragging him back here. There were now more cars in the driveway including another patrol car and one she imagined belonged to the homicide detectives.

Let it go. Leave it to the experts.

She took John's hand. "On reflection, the authorities are capable of solving this without me."

The front door swung open and Bertie blocked the doorway. He'd aged, if that was possible, since they'd last seen him. No wonder.

"You might as well come in instead of standing out here arguing."

"Oh, we weren't arguing. Just debating whether we are even needed." Daphne said.

"They're gonna arrest Lisa so come and join the party." He shuffled down the hallway.

"We can go." Daphne whispered, but John shook his head and led the way inside.

They followed Bertie to the living room, where Matty nodded to them from beside two plainclothes officers who were speaking with Bob. Lisa perched on the arm of a sofa and grinned at Daphne. For someone about to be arrested she was calm. But Margaret was not, pacing the floor with tears rolling down her cheeks.

Wherever Dempster had been earlier, he was here now, bleary eyes barely flicking to the newcomers from his seat in the furthest corner of the room. He sipped from a bottle of water.

The detectives stepped away from Bob to speak with Matty. All three glanced at Daphne and John and then to Lisa. Matty said something and the younger of the detectives nodded then directed his attention to Lisa.

"Ms Brooker—"

"Mrs Tanning."

"Sorry. Mrs Tanning, if you have nothing more to say at this time, we intend to take you into custody for further questioning. An attorney may be present and—"

"Sorry to interrupt again, but maybe you should ask Mrs Jones if she thinks I did it?" Lisa tilted her head and softened her voice as she leaned forward a fraction. "Another moment or two won't change anything, will it…Captain?"

Matty smirked as the 'captain' glanced at the other detective but didn't bother to correct Lisa's obvious attempt at flattery or flirting. Or both.

"Mrs Jones was here when Steve died and she helped us all. She also came here this morning at my request when I was...flustered and upset by finding my great-aunt, and she has a lot of experience solving crimes."

What? I do?

The eyes of every person in the room shot to Daphne and her legs shook. Just a little.

"I...er, um, no I have helped with a crime investigation back in our home town but I'm not any kind of expert."

"You've been most helpful so far, Mrs Jones." Matty said. "We may need an interview about the events from yesterday by the pool as well as what you observed earlier today in the paddock."

"And I'm happy to assist. But if you want to arrest somebody why not the killer?"

Margaret, who'd stopped pacing and was drying her eyes with tissues, grabbed Bob's arm.

"Do you know who the killer is, Mrs Jones?" This was the older of the detectives. "Or is it speculation?"

Daphne drew in a long breath as her eyes darted from face to face until back on the detective. "That's for you to decide, but I do believe I know. And the person might well be in this very room with us."

A KILLER REVEALED?

The silence dragged until the older detective crossed to the living room door and closed it, before leaning against the timber with his arms folded. This simple action stirred the occupants and Daphne was well aware all three police officers were taking mental notes.

Bob stood to his full height and pushed his chest out. Not a word passed his lips, but his defensive appeared to startle Margaret, who released his arm as if it burned. She sank onto the sofa near her daughter.

"The killer is in this room?" Her eyes moved from person to person.

Lisa made herself more comfortable on her perch and drew in air through pursed lips. Margaret reached for her hand but Lisa brushed it away a bit impatiently.

With a grin, Bertie wandered to the window and pushed aside the lacy curtain to look outside. Hopefully, he wasn't losing himself at this important time but at least he wasn't trying to take himself off for a walk.

Still in his seat in the corner, Dempster put the lid on the bottle of water and stared at Daphne. Unwavering. Curious even.

"So, Mrs Jones, when you say the killer may be in this room, can you specify whose killer?" Matty asked. He took his notepad out. "We may have more than one."

What have you got yourself into, Daph?

She touched her lips with the tip of her tongue. A dry mouth would stop the words and for once, she needed them to come out in a way which made sense to every person in the room. Especially the police officers. They'd granted her a rare opportunity to speak her mind and if she messed up, the killer would have valuable information and potentially be free to cover their tracks. Beside her, John smiled in encouragement.

"I believe the killer of Steve and the killer of Gina are one and the same person. Since the day of poor Steve's tragedy, I've made extensive notes based upon my observations. The past few days have exposed me to a number of interesting pieces of information. Overheard conversations, local history, legal records. And watching how people interact and how they speak to each other."

"Sounds like spying. We invited you into our home and you spy on us." Bob ran a finger around the neckline of the business shirt beneath his black suit. Did he ever wear anything else?

"Although spying sounds awfully interesting, I did nothing of the sort. Every person in here has volunteered snippets of gossip, opinion, and outright statements. And almost all were unsolicited."

"Rubbish. What have I said to you that would make me a suspect?" Bob demanded.

"Let me see. You called Steve 'a little rat' in front of me. Sorry, Lisa."

"I've heard him say it enough." Lisa said.

Daphne continued. "You told me you were unhappy about the wedding and having all the guests in your home."

He snorted. "*That* is your evidence?"

"I understand you insisted the pool tiles be polished the day before the wedding which would have made the footing slippery. Easier to push someone into the pool."

"True. You did insist I redo them." Dempster piped up. "They didn't need it."

Bob glared at him.

"There's more but I can't see you as either the killer or the brains behind it."

Daphne changed her focus to Margaret, whose fingers worked overtime on a tissue, shredding it into tiny strips.

"Margaret, you told me you didn't like Steve. I heard you say you wished Lisa would stop putting you through all the weddings. And that the problem was Lisa's taste in husbands. Again, sorry Lisa."

This time Lisa didn't respond. Her body stiffened and her mouth was clamped shut.

"But like with Bob, you are not the killer or the brains behind it."

"Who has brains?" Bertie left the window and sat beside Margaret on the sofa. "Not Lisa. I love her, but she lets people walk all over her. Not real smart if you ask me."

"Thanks, Gramps."

He didn't seem to care, smiling to himself as he played with the buttons on his shirt.

Matty cleared his throat to get the attention back on himself. "Mrs Jones, this is very enlightening, but so far you're excluding people rather than telling us who you think is behind the deaths of Steve and Gina. Lisa had blood on her hands when we arrived. She'd interfered with the crime scene. Yet you implied Lisa is not responsible."

"I can understand Lisa being a suspect. And in both

deaths." Daphne decided she'd apologised to Lisa enough and instead kept her eyes on Matty. "Not only were her two previous husbands in the grave, but now a third one was dead. All related by blood to each other and there is a feud between both families which might offer motive. Steve was quite rude to her during the ceremony which for some people might tip them over the edge."

"My daughter is not a killer!" Margaret burst into tears.

"Oh, for goodness' sake, Mum. You're sounding like me now." Lisa reached for a box of tissues on a coffee table and dropped them in her mother's lap.

"At the farewell ceremony yesterday, Gina was horrible to Lisa. Horrible to a few people. And Lisa? You gave back as good as you got. I recall you said you'd never forgive her for making sure Steve's family didn't attend the wedding. How better to reinforce your feelings than with a steak knife in her back?"

Oh my. You are on a roll!

"But...but I didn't kill anyone." There it was. The waver in the voice.

Before this turned into a Lisa pity party, Daphne moved on. Two left.

A SHOCK CONFESSION

"I've known the family for a long time, Mrs Jones. Do any of them even look like killers?" Dempster asked.

"But what does a killer look like? Young or older? Quick to anger..." Daphne glanced at Lisa, who averted her eyes. "or quick to disappear?" This was directed at Bertie, who nodded with a somewhat vacant expression. He was clearly off somewhere in his mind. "For many reasons I excluded Lisa, not the least being her visibility at the wedding. She simply had no chance to kill Steve. And, in my humble opinion, she had no motive strong enough to drive her to do so."

Dempster remained still apart from the fingers of one hand tapping on the arm of the chair.

After a quick breath, Daphne continued. "Time for me to be honest. I thought Gina was behind this all. That she was the brains. And I still do."

"My sister? No brains there." Bertie offered with a small chuckle. "Where is Gina?" Margaret patted his arm.

"Gina was a proud woman and an even prouder Brooker, in my estimation." Daphne said.

Everyone nodded, even Matty.

"She had no time for the Tanning family. More than that, she was old enough to remember handed down stories of the original family feud. Two men who fought over a woman, both losing their lives in the process. Friends who left behind their children with no parents. Gina may have heard the story from her own grandparents and parents. Do you remember the story, Bertie?"

He nodded. "I grew up knowing no Tanning is a good one. Wasn't true though."

"You had a business deal with Toby Tanning."

"Good partner. Good friend. Until Bob started nosing around and making accusations." Bertie sighed deeply and returned to his buttons.

Bob spluttered. "Nosing around! I acted on advice from your own sister."

All heads—apart from Bertie's—swung to Bob. This was a new detail.

"Gina told me to take a look. You weren't even using a bookkeeper and money was disappearing with no record. She was worried when she heard you and Tanning discuss buying out the parts shop and she was right. That was once a thriving little business and went under thanks to you and Tanning."

Bertie didn't respond. In fact, he hummed beneath his breath.

Bob clenched his hands then strode to a liquor cabinet and poured himself a glass of something. After swallowing the contents, he leaned against the wall and glared at everyone.

"This reinforces Gina's track record of anti-Tanning activities. I have a whole list of them in my notebook. Obviously, this is for the police to investigate, but my belief is that Gina is responsible for the deaths of Steve, and quite possibly Sam and Shane."

Lisa jumped to her feet. "She what?"

Matty shook his head. "Those deaths were ruled accidental. And Gina wasn't even in the country when Shane died."

Sink or swim, Daph.

Daphne gestured to the corner. "But Dempster was."

"Huh?" Dempster's mouth dropped open.

"But he's been with us for years!" Margaret squealed.

"Hired him myself. What a load of rubbish." Bob helped himself to more liquor.

The detective near Matty opened his phone and tapped away.

Dempster got to his feet. "If you're talking about when the branch fell then yeah, I was there. Worst day ever."

Lisa stalked across the room to stand in front of Dempster. "For Shane!"

"Yeah. And me. Was an accident."

Daphne took control back. "You may have noticed that Gina was stabbed in the back. Quite literally. No way she did that to herself but it doesn't mean she wasn't behind the other murders. I've been mentioning the killer and the brains behind the killer. Two different people. Yesterday Gina stated she was going to speak to the police. Nobody knew what about...or did they? I think Gina had an accomplice. Someone to do the dirty work."

"Not me. I'm clean as a whistle." Dempster attempted to slide past Lisa, but she grabbed his arms and screamed at him.

"What did you do to my husbands? Did you kill my boys?"

All three police reacted as one and surrounded Lisa and Dempster. A minute later Lisa was escorted back to the sofa by Matty, while Dempster stood with the detectives on either side of him.

Daphne fanned her face with her hand. John put his hand on the middle of her back and his support, his gentle reminder he was close, let her push away the little voice in her head telling her she was being cruel. Upsetting innocent people. Making a scene.

You've come a long way, Daph.

What she was doing was standing up for what was right.

"Why would I kill anyone?" Dempster whined. "I just work here."

The older detective watched Daphne, his face unreadable. She'd better get a hurry on.

"Dempster, I think you want more than just to work here. I think you believe you have a claim on the Brooker name and any wealth that comes with. Is it true you descend from Mary Smith?"

The man's eyes widened.

"Just who is Mary Smith and how is this relevant?" Bob sounded a bit slurred and from the look of it was onto his third drink.

"She was the wife of your own ancestor, Richard Brooker. The woman who left him to live with Joseph Tanning. The person the men fought over. And she was carrying a child when she vanished. Probably Richard's. Genealogy records point to Dempster being her descendant."

"But I—" Dempster started.

"It is all true." Margaret got to her feet and faced Daphne. "Clever, aren't you? Dempster came here years ago demanding he be acknowledged as a Brooker. With his hand out. He wanted what wasn't his and when I told him some truths he didn't take kindly to it. Thought I'd need to call the police. Thank goodness Bertie arrived and sorted him out."

"Mum? You never said anything to me."

"Or to me." Bob put down his drink as the colour drained from his face. "Is Dempster my relative?"

"Hello. I'm right here." Dempster waved. "But your wife is nuts. I'm not violent. I was disappointed when she said the

Brooker estate was virtually gone and any money was from her side of the family."

Bob stumbled his way across the room to the other man. The older detective held up a hand to stop him getting any closer so he planted his feet and peered at Dempster. "You look a bit like a Brooker. Never saw it before."

"Bob! You're missing the point. He wanted to waltz in here and take our property. Become part of our family. Steal from us the way you say the Tannings do." Margaret wrung her hands together. "Bertie stopped him from pursuing his ridiculous claim."

"Perhaps, Bertie can shed some light...where's Bertie?" Daphne asked. She gazed around the room. His spot on the sofa was empty. He wasn't back at the window. And when she glanced behind herself, the door was ajar.

MORE THAN MISSING

"I'll go and find him." Dempster took a step but the hand of one of the detectives stopped him.

"Not just yet. We'll hear out Mrs Jones and then locate Mr Brooker."

Bob returned to the liquor cabinet. "Silly old man won't be far. Trust him to wander off when we need answers."

"Margaret, what did Bertie do to placate Dempster all those years ago?" Daphne asked. "And why not tell the family about his true identity?"

The other woman turned bright red and hung her head. "I didn't want him here. I'm ashamed of myself for not extending a welcome but Lisa had spent a lot of money on building the house and our lives were going so well." She raised her eyes in Dempster's direction. "I am sorry, Dempster. I treated you unfairly."

Dempster shrugged. His usual friendly manner was gone. His eyes had narrowed and there was a wariness about him Daphne had never noticed before. Funny how people show themselves when under pressure.

"As for what Bertie did? Well, he offered him a job. Said

we needed someone to help around the garden and pool. At first it was a couple of days a week and then Bertie and Dempster started going fishing together and before I knew it, Bertie wanted him living in the old caravan."

"And you were okay with that?"

"Not at all. But Dempster gave me a choice. Give in to Bertie's idea or else Dempster would tell everyone he was related and start legal action. He didn't care if he only got a small piece of the pie, as I recall him putting it." Shoulders down, Margaret returned to the sofa and plonked down.

The younger detective checked his phone and showed it to his partner. Dempster craned his neck to see but they stepped away from him. His eyes darted to the door as if judging how fast he could reach it. The muscle in his cheek twitched. John must have noticed for he casually closed the door again and as the detective had, leaned against it. Dempster shot him a look of such malice that Daphne shivered. Thank goodness there were three police officers in the room.

The older detective spoke. "We've had an officer walk down to the caravan. He has observed the trace of a blood-like substance on one of the steps."

Everyone looked at Dempster's feet, which wore socks, but no footwear.

Margaret pointed to the back of the house. "He knows to take his boots off before entering."

"We'll collect them on our way to the caravan. Dempster Smith, we would appreciate your co-operation in the investigation of the death of—"

Dempster made a dash for the door and Matty flew across the room, stopping him a foot or two away from John ,who hadn't moved an inch and smiled at Daphne.

She'd had about enough now. This was too nerve-wracking for words.

A couple of minutes later, Dempster was in handcuffs being escorted down the hallway. Matty lingered.

"Mrs Jones, you have great insight. But what made you believe Dempster and Gina had an arrangement?"

"Gina hated the Tannings. She believed the old adage of them always stealing from the Brookers. Dempster was someone she could manipulate based on his disappointment at being an outcast thanks to the action of Joseph Tanning all those decades ago. At least, that's my theory, for what it's worth."

Bob was sitting beside Margaret, holding her hand. "You should have said something, Mags. Not put up with being bullied into silence."

A tear rolled down Margaret's face.

Lisa collected the tissue box again and kneeled in front of her mother. "We'll get through this. You did nothing wrong, Mamma."

Matty stepped into the hallway and Daphne could see no reason to stay with the Brookers. She and John closed the door behind themselves.

"What happens now?"

"There's a lot to investigate. Crime scene is still on its way so the body is staying where it is for now. Dempster will be questioned at the station and I imagine formally charged for Gina's murder. And I'm going to ask the detectives if it is worth looking at the deaths of Shane and Sam again."

A pleasant warmth spread through Daphne. If some good came of her efforts—hers and John's—then it balanced out the worry and upset. The ruin of the wedding might be redeemed a little.

John's phone rang. "Looks like the number from the tyre people. I'll go answer it."

"Matty, are we able to leave? Town, I mean?"

"I think we've kept you here long enough." He smiled. "We

will need a statement but you can make it in your next town. Just let me know once you are there and I'll arrange it."

"Do you need us to help look for Bertie?"

"Can't imagine he's gone too far. Looks like John's waving to you."

"Then I'll say goodbye. And thank you for allowing me to speak."

"You've been persistent," he grinned. "From the beginning you told me you had suspicions and it turns out you were right."

NOT QUITE DONE

"I don't know if being a celebrant is right for you, doll."

Daphne had gazed out of the window since they'd driven away from the Brooker residence. She'd not spoken once but her body language reassured John she was simply processing and no longer stressing.

"You may be right." She said, without looking at him. "Not certain I can perform another wedding without expecting a tragedy."

"Hm. Not what I meant."

"I wouldn't be surprised if more clients cancelled."

"Doubt it. If anything you should increase your fee."

Now she did turn her head.

"You've done something amazing today, Daph. Solved a crime and with a bit of luck, put a criminal behind bars. Not every bride and groom can say they were married by a celebrant sleuth."

The corners of Daphne's mouth lifted and her eyes twinkled. "Celebrant sleuth. Has a nice ring to it."

"That's my girl. You did good. And now we're getting new tyres and can finally get back on the road. Time to begin planning the next ceremony. And what we'll have for dinner tonight."

On cue, his stomach rumbled and they both laughed.

"You didn't even get to have cookies for breakfast, let alone a real one. I'll make us a nice lunch while the tyres are being done. What do you fancy?"

He fancied being by a river fishing, but not in this town. Somewhere far from criminals and vandals.

"John?"

"Sorry, love. Anything at all. As long as we eat lunch together and without interruptions, I'll be a happy man."

She smiled. "I'm not about to let anyone or anything interrupt our time together for quite a while."

THE INTENTION WAS good but there was almost no food left in the caravan and it would take ages to defrost anything. Grabbing her handbag and a shopping bag, she went to find John.

He was getting Bluebell ready to be lifted enough to change her tyres. "They'll be along in the next few minutes." He held chocks in either hand.

"I'm going to walk to town and find us some lunch, love. How about some pies from the bakery?"

John dropped an absent-minded kiss on her forehead. "Take the car."

"I think a short walk will do me good. Back soon."

In the distance a work truck approached. Daphne estimated she'd be back before they finished if she got a move on. Ten minutes either way and a bit of time to shop. She might drop in and say goodbye to Maurice at the newspaper. And thank him for his part in helping her reach the conclusion of Gina and Dempster being responsible for at least

Steve's murder.

Something didn't sit right with Daphne. As much as Dempster denied it, she was confident he was the brawn behind the brains. With his medical background, hatred of the Tannings, and physical match, it all fitted. But there was more to this and it had to tie in with the deaths of Shane and Sam. Yet Gina had been out of the picture for at least one of those deaths.

At the first clump of trees, where the boot prints were still visible in the dried dirt, Daphne looked back to Bluebell. John chatted to one of the tyre fitters while a second man rolled the new tyres off the back of their truck. Had it been Dempster standing here the other night? Plotting to damage Bluebell? Why though? At the time, Daphne didn't recall even speaking to him, letting alone suspecting him. What reason would he have to watch her?

With a shudder, she got going. No point worrying over what might have happened. Dempster was in custody and with Gina dead, the killings would stop.

Or will they?

"If the police come calling just remember you forced me to do this." Those were Gina's last words to Bertie, overheard by their family, friends, Dempster, and Daphne. A threat to anyone who had something to hide, after she'd reminded them earlier of her knowledge of 'torrid family secrets'. She might be one of those people who stored information on people in order to blackmail them.

"But why would you bring the police into it?" Daphne stopped again. "If you were the brains then you'd go to jail as well."

Her gut was churning. What had she missed? Was there a chance Gina was not Dempster's accomplice? She needed her notes. A fresh look at them based on the new information from this morning. But first she had to buy lunch and then she could have another read.

The bridge was up ahead and as she closed in on it, Daphne jumped as a large thicket of reeds rustled and a tall, thin figure emerged from its centre. The person wore a hoodie and wiped their hands down their front, leaving white streaks, then sauntered onto the bridge as if that was normal behaviour.

Daphne hurried to the spot the person had stood. A trail of white liquid which looked like paint, led towards the river and Daphne forced her way through the reeds.

Too far into the river for her to reach, a white tub slowly submerged. An open tub with the word 'Poison' on its side. Thick white liquid seeped into the river and just before it sank, a small black object floated out. A phone.

Gina's phone?

Where was the person who'd done this? Daphne's eyes shot back to the bridge and there, heading towards town, the person strolled along. Not a care in the world. She climbed back through the reeds, her fingers in her handbag grasping for her phone. Stopping long enough to dial, Daphne held the phone to her ear and snuck onto the bridge.

"John. It's me. Daphne. I'm following the real brains. Not Gina. But someone else. Get the police. They threw the missing phone in the river. Bluebell's side of the bridge to town. Hurry." She hung up. He had to get the message. She risked taking a photo of the tub which was visible under the surface. The white cloud around it should help the police locate it. That done, she began to dial the police and started up the bridge. Nobody was in sight.

She shoved the phone away and began to run.

At the crest of the bridge she spotted the person almost at the far end. They glanced back and stopped. The face was impossible to see from this distance but she knew they recognised her when they turned and sprinted away.

"Staaap!"

What was meant to be an authoritative command sounded like the screech of an angry bird. And did nothing other than draw the attention of a group of women—all dressed in fitness wear—doing star jumps partway down the bridge. As Daphne puffed her way past them, she sang out, "Call the police. I'm in pursuit!"

"You're going to pop those buttons, honey." One woman said.

"Or have a coronary." Another added.

Laughter followed Daphne. Her head dropped for an instant and her legs faltered. But there was no time for being sorry for herself.

She reached the bottom of the bridge, grabbing a post to help her around the corner and onto the path. "There you are!"

The figure was still too far ahead to identify.

Sweat poured down Daphne's neck.

It was getting hotter with every painful step.

The path weaved through trees, offering a welcome respite from the sun.

But the hooded figure was out of sight.

Faster, Daph. Don't let them escape.

She might have been in the wilderness with not a soul around between the dense undergrowth on either side and the canopy above the winding track. It suddenly split in two around a large gum tree.

Daphne took the left path and ran straight into another body.

Her feet slid from beneath her.

The ground rose.

With a sickening 'thud' she hit the path.

Silence.

A breath. Hers.

And a moan. Not hers.

Daphne turned over onto all fours and used the trunk of the tree to help her up. The hooded figure was a bit further away and took a moment to stand, straightening with another moan. A male moan. Blood seeped through the fabric of the hoodie down his left arm, which hung at his side.

For a moment they got their respective breaths back.

They were alone.

She was alone with the killer.

The person pushed back the hood with their good arm.

"You." Daphne gasped.

"Me. And now you know who I am."

Bertie grinned at Daphne. It might have been a chance meeting on a spring day in a peaceful country town.

Between a killer and their pursuer.

THE ARRANGEMENT

"Why, Bertie?"

"Interesting question, Mrs Jones. Why run? Why dispose of the evidence? Or why dispatch people who try to harm my family?"

The man standing before Daphne was a far cry from the elderly person whose memory led him astray. His eyes were sharp. His body strong, apart from his damaged arm. Old, yes, but strong. What an odd thing to remember but his photographs and trophies had been in front of Daphne every time she'd entered the Brooker house. He'd been a runner. A champion runner.

"You don't have dementia."

He chuckled. "They all think I do. Made it easy to do what I wanted."

Daphne shifted her weight. The impact of the fall left her ankle throbbing. The earlier churning in her stomach was replaced by a cold and heavy stone. Was she the next victim?

How had she missed the clues?

As if reading her mind, Bertie's smile vanished and he took a step forward. And a second. Daphne's back was against the tree trunk and her eyes darted around. Why wasn't anyone around to help?

"Gina wasn't meant to die. Silly woman talking about going to the police must have freaked out Dempster but she was my sister. He had no right."

With only a few feet between them, the grief in Bertie's eyes was real and in spite of her fear, Daphne felt for him. But more for Gina.

"I'm sorry I accused her. But I don't understand how Dempster got to Steve that day. Gina said she'd seen you both on the other side of the property."

"She lied. Never had anything to do with the arrangement, but she knew enough and we always protected each other. Until I didn't."

In the distance, a siren sounded. Bertie's eyes roamed, settling on a short, thick fallen branch and then back at Daphne.

A shiver ran through her body. "Um… The arrangement?"

"Nobody else in the world knows. Only Demps and me. And Gina knew bits. So if I tell you, it's our secret." He grimaced and glanced at his left arm. The blood now dripped beneath the sleeve onto his fingers, which were motionless. "That's annoying."

Bertie shuffled to the fallen branch. He leaned down, his fingertips touching the bark.

Daphne edged away from the gum tree. "No point harming me. Your blood is all over the ground and you'll be in jail before you know it."

With a groan, Bertie straightened. His hand was empty. "Just wanted something to lean on." He managed a short laugh. "I'm the brains, remember. Not the brawn."

"What if we get you some help."

"I'm past help. Might use the tree though to prop me up."

Daphne hobbled further away. She wasn't about to let

him near her and if she had to, she would scream the place down. He sighed as he rested against the trunk.

"What arrangement did you have with Dempster?"

"Our secret, right?"

With a nod, Daphne apologised to him in her mind. She'd break his trust the minute she could. The siren had stopped wailing.

"Dempster and I were a lot alike. He grew up hating a family he'd never met. The Tannings. He'd been told the same stories I was. Joseph Tanning stole Mary from our ancestor. And every Tanning since then followed suit. Bunch of liars and thieves." He ground the words out.

"But you said Toby was your friend."

"He was useful. I had it under control and was gradually squirrelling away every dollar he'd invested in it. Gina and Bob ruined everything but I had enough money hidden in a safe place to partly rebuild the Brooker wealth."

An embezzler. Was it all about money?

Bertie continued, speaking faster as if telling his story for the first time. "Dempster came along when I was unsure of my next move. Money was hidden. Still is. Lisa was spending hers and lots of it was on me and my family. Wasn't about to stop her. But then she married one of them."

"Sam Tanning?"

"Yup. And I knew time was running before they started a family because the minute they had a kid all the money would flow away from me and mine. Bob was all I had left and then Demps came along. Not my grandson but the nearest thing I'd ever have and he'd been done out of a lifetime of his rightful Brooker name. So we brokered an arrangement to stop anyone who tried to take away my legacy."

There was movement further up the path, behind Bertie

and the tree. Police uniforms appearing and disappearing through the bushes.

Bertie stopped talking and his eyes closed. His skin was a sickly shade of grey and the bleeding hadn't slowed.

"Bertie? You told me you love Lisa."

He opened his eyes and his lips turned up. "She's a good girl. A bit emotional and makes bad decisions but yes, I love her."

"Then why would you kill her husbands? And don't remind me it is because of some legacy or for revenge." Daphne lifted her chin. "You and Dempster took away her happiness. What makes you any different from the Tannings?"

His mouth opened and closed. A shaking began in his legs, getting stronger by the second until they started to buckle. Daphne managed to reach him before he collapsed, getting his good arm over her shoulder and using all her strength to keep him upright.

"A little help!" she cried out.

He dropped his head so his mouth was close to her ear. "I was a fool. Tell Lisa I'm sorry." As his body went limp, strong arms caught him. Matty was there.

IN THE REAR VIEW MIRROR

"I promised you we'd leave this town today, and I'm keeping to my promise." John held Daphne's hand so tight it hurt but she wasn't letting go.

The last few hours were dreamlike, which might also be in part due to some painkillers the local doctor gave her after ensuring her ankle wasn't broken. Painkillers and anti-inflammatories plus instructions to rest.

Bluebell was fully operational and ready to leave, but a call from Matty delayed their departure again. John had agreed to wait for half an hour and then he was taking his wife away from Little Bridges once and for all. They sat inside Bluebell to wait, finishing the last of the cookies with some apple cider. Lunch hadn't happened and they'd both decided to give up on finding a meal until on the road.

"I wonder how Bertie is." Daphne hadn't stopped thinking about him since the paramedics strapped him onto a stretcher and took him to hospital with a police escort.

"I'm more concerned about you, my love." John finally released her hand to refill their glasses and glanced out of the open door. "You should have waited for help."

Daphne smiled. "Do you remember back home when that awful man broke into our house and I ran down the road to see what kind of car he had?"

"How could I forget? But at least then you were on a street where people could see you, not camouflaged by trees and bushes. Thank goodness those women did as you asked and phoned the police."

"Oh. Them."

"Why?"

Would they have stopped a killer?

She shook her head. "Doesn't matter."

"And I heard your message and must have phoned the police a couple of minutes later and thank goodness Matty and Leading Senior Constable Barber knew the general area you were in. Had no idea I could still run so fast!"

The patrol car parked next to the open door.

"Hopefully, he doesn't want another statement." John said.

Apart from the visit to the doctor, Daphne had spent quite a long time making a full statement at the police station. With Bertie's confession the homicide detectives had more to investigate.

"Afternoon. Thanks for hanging around." Matty appeared in the doorway. "May I?"

"Come on in. Iced tea?" Daphne offered, moving over to make room for him to sit. John collected a fresh glass and poured a drink before Matty could reply.

"I have some news. Thanks for this." He sat. "Bertie is undergoing surgery but expected to recover. We were able to retrieve the tub from the river and the phone and yes, it is the one stolen from Gina and used to lure Steve to the pool."

Tears prickled at the back of Daphne's eyes as a sudden wave of relief washed away the tension and stress of the past few days. She didn't speak for fear of crying, but tapped her hands together in a discreet clap. If Matty noticed her emotional response he was too polite to say anything but John caught her eye and smiled.

"We've formerly charged Dempster with two counts of first degree murder pending other charges. He has admitted to stabbing Steve, pushing him into the pool and then using the hose to wash the obvious blood into the water. He hid in the cleaning room until Steve was found. The Brooker and Tanning families have both expressed gratitude to you and asked me to pass that on."

"I would imagine much of this is a shock to the Brookers. Their patriarch behind such heinous crimes for the sake of money and his family name." John said. "Hopefully, they'll move on in time and at least no more murders."

Matty nodded. "There's one more thing. We found the person responsible for slashing your tyres. They've been charged on summons and have already offered to make full restitution for the cost of replacing them. I'd suggest wait until the offer is formerly made and then counter offer to cover your time and any other expenses. Sadly, that's the best way for this person to learn."

"Who did it?" Daphne found her voice. "I thought it was Dempster."

"No. It was Lloyd."

Daphne gasped.

"He was angry at the attention he got from your report and decided to pay you back. Now, he really has to pay you back."

She'd known Lloyd wasn't a nice person. Not one to be happy at another's misfortune, Daphne nevertheless enjoyed a moment of glee. Nice to see swift justice done.

Matty finished his drink and stood. "Time to let you both get on your way."

"At last." John said, but there was no malice in his tone.

He offered his hand and Matty shook it before turning his gaze onto Daphne.

"We might have got off on the wrong foot, but I've come to respect you, Mrs Jones. You've got good instincts. But no more getting in the way of trouble. Okay?"

"I'll see you out."

The men climbed out and Daphne opened her notebook to a new page to write her final words about Little Bridges.

Family matters but when money and pride become more important, terrible decisions are made. The Brooker and Tanning families may never be friends, but at least they now have one common enemy—the past and its influence. If they can put that behind them then there is a chance for a better future.

"Ready, love?" John was back inside and held out his hand. "Let's get you into the car and we can be off."

"No last minute shopping? No people to say goodbye to?" she teased, letting him help her out of Bluebell.

"I don't think I'll answer that one." John wrapped Daphne in his arms. "There's only one picture I want in my head of this town."

Daphne leaned back and kissed his lips. "Little Bridges in the rear vision mirror?"

He answered with a kiss in return.

NEXT... THE SHADOW OF DAPH

The forest town of Shady Bend is known for its crafts, preserves, and local produce. It is not known for disappearing bodies let alone a mysterious spate of crimes!

Daphne came to officiate a funeral for Edwina Drinkwater but in a shocking twist, the deceased vanishes before making it to the grave. The sudden death of a mourner who kept records of other people's indiscretions evokes Daphne's inner sleuth. Was the murder payback?

Who has hidden Edwina's remains? Was it the neighbour who wants her land, the disgraced local doctor, or her fiercest competitor in the world of preserves and jams?

With judging underway at the local country show, the suspects come together all determined to obtain Edwina's famous secret sauce recipe. But as the body count rises, Daphne is the only person standing between the killer and the truth.

AFTERWORD

I love writing Australian stories. There are differences in spelling and terminology between Aussie and US for example, but keeping them 'Aussie' brings them to life.

The celebrant/officiant role Daphne undertakes is fictional with a factual basis, so there will be some variation from the role of a real celebrant, particularly in other countries.

A quick word about my support team. My family of course, who are always there for me. Nas, my editor and dear friend, is my rock. Jade, who created this cute cover, makes me laugh myself silly sometimes. I admire her talent so much. Marcia Ray (Batton), Belinda Missen, Alison Stuart, Savannah Blaize, Rozzi Bazzani, Janeen O'Connell, Jenny Lynch, and Louise Guy - you all were there when I needed you. And so many other gorgeous people who are friends near or far. And to all the wonderful readers? I love you all.

ABOUT THE AUTHOR

Phillipa lives just outside a beautiful town in country Victoria, Australia. She also lives in the many worlds of her imagination and stockpiles stories beside her laptop.

Apart from her family, Phillipa's great loves include the ocean, music, reading, the garden, and animals of all kinds.

To keep in touch, follow Phillipa on Facebook or other social media, or join her newsletter via the form on her website.

WWW.PHILLIPACLARK.COM

THREE SERIES IN ONE WORLD

Twelve books across three series - all connected by characters, themes, and lots of heart...

Rivers End came first. Four main books and three companion stories, revolving around old secrets in a tiny seaside town. It is part historical mystery romance, part contemporary women's fiction, and a whole lot of small town values.

The Charlotte Dean Mysteries are set a few hours away from Rivers End, inland among old forests and striking landscapes. Kingfisher Falls is a town with many secrets and Charlotte -who first appeared in Rivers End - finds herself in the middle of solving them. A mix of traditional and cozy mystery with a gentle romance (or two).

The Daphne Jones Mysteries continue the story of Daphne and John, who were supporting characters in all the Rivers End books and appear in one of Charlotte's. They have retired and travel in their cute caravan, Bluebell, to allow

Daphne to officiate weddings and funerals. With her inner sleuth on high alert there is always something exciting going on. This series is cozy mystery but with a strong sense of family.

Check Phillipa's website for the reading order of this world set in the beautiful rural countryside of Victoria, Australia.

In addition, Phillipa writes standalone crime suspense books, fantasy, and also a non-fiction happiness book.

Printed in Great Britain
by Amazon

81140732R00140